'Now you need someone to satisfy your needs.'

Emily turned her head and opened her eyes. His head was close, resting on the cushion right by hers. 'What makes you think I haven't got someone already?'

'If you did, you wouldn't be looking at me with those hungry eyes.'

She lifted her head, a little on her dignity. 'You don't need to lay it on with a trowel, Luca. I'm not completely inexperienced.'

'Only *relatively—si*?' He laughed. 'What was he? Some young fool who wouldn't know how to give pleasure to a woman even if she gave him step-by-step instructions and a map showing the way?'

She felt the blush covering her cheeks and neck, and she shut her eyes again to pretend it wasn't happening. He'd been exactly like that.

'Emily. I can offer you nothing but a memory.' His voice was a little strained. 'But I think it would be some memory.'

BETWEEN THE ITALIAN'S SHEETS

BY
NATALIE ANDERSON

MILLS & BOON®
MODERN
Heat™

All the characters in this book have no existence outside the imagination of the author, and have no relation whatsoever to anyone bearing the same name or names. They are not even distantly inspired by any individual known or unknown to the author, and all the incidents are pure invention.

First published in Great Britain 2009
Harlequin Mills & Boon Limited,
Eton House, 18-24 Paradise Road, Richmond, Surrey TW9 1SR

© Natalie Anderson 2009

ISBN: 978 0 263 87242 2

Set in Times Roman 10½ on 13½ pt
171-0609-45049

Printed and bound in Spain
by Litografia Rosés, S.A., Barcelona

Possibly the only librarian who got told off herself for talking too much, **Natalie Anderson** decided writing books might be more fun than shelving them—and, boy, is it that! Especially writing romance—it's the realisation of a lifetime dream, kick-started by many an afternoon spent devouring Grandma's Mills & Boons®... She lives in New Zealand, with her husband and four gorgeous-but-exhausting children. Swing by her website any time—she'd love to hear from you: www.natalie-anderson.com

Recent titles by the same author:

PLEASURED IN THE PLAYBOY'S PENTHOUSE
BOUGHT: ONE NIGHT, ONE MARRIAGE
PLEASURED BY THE SECRET MILLIONAIRE

For Rosie and Simon.
You two have the most incredible generosity,
kindness and sheer zest for life. Our holiday in London
at Casa King-Currie was amazing—every moment fun
and relaxing and memorable. Luca and Emily's story
would never have come out into the light if it hadn't
been for the break you enabled us to have,
and for that I really, really thank you.

CHAPTER ONE

ARROGANCE personified. Emily stared at him, her temper going from sizzling to spitting hot. He stood right in front of her, with the height of a basketball star, and shoulders the breadth of a rugby prop. A man mountain, a mighty example of the male in physical prime. Totally obscuring her view. Totally commanding attention.

Typical.

Worse than that, he had one of those fancy phone gadgets that did everything—not merely phone calls, but music, web connection, camera—the works. And every time he pushed the buttons they beeped. Loudly. The overture was about to begin, Emily found the rapid succession of beeps incredibly annoying.

Pointedly, she cleared her throat.

She had not spent the last year working crazy hours, scrimping and saving every last cent to get her sister and herself all the way to Italy and to this fabulous opera only for the moment to be ruined by some selfish jerk who thought his social life was more important than the live performance about to unfold. More important than showing some respect to the other people there who wanted to appreciate the evening.

She cleared her throat again.

Fractionally he turned, threw a quick glance her way, but the beeping didn't stop. Rather it was the cacophony of trills and fragments of well-known phrases that ceased as under the direction of the lead violinist the orchestra stilled. Then came the lone note from the oboe to which the other instruments would tune. But did that stop him? No. The purity of the sound was shattered by the relentless beeping.

Any minute now the conductor would walk out and applause would greet him. Beeps didn't constitute applause. Beeps were annoying. And she couldn't *see* through him.

She glared at his back now as well as clearing her throat once more. A tailored jacket hung from those doorframe-wide shoulders, one hand on his hip pulling the jacket back, emphasising the narrowing of his torso to a slim waist and hips. She knew there were serious muscles under the white shirt and dark trousers. She'd watched as he'd walked up from the super-expensive seats. He was hard not to notice, taller than almost all the people there. From the front she'd seen the way his shirt neatly tucked into his trousers with not an ounce of anything unnecessary—like fat—rippling the smooth, straight stretch of white cotton. Well dressed, good-looking, so sophisticated and cool in this hot and crowded space. She figured he'd come up so as not to disturb those in his own elite strata—no, he'd conduct his business and bother the plebs up in the cheap seats.

One of the waiters came past, singing his way through the crowd for one final time before he'd quieten for the spectacle, tormenting her with his cry.

'Bebite! Acqua! Cola! Vino bianca! Vino rosso! Bebite…'

She'd go for all those drinks right now. She was hot. She was thirsty. She was irritated.

This time she coughed.

Where on earth was Kate? What was taking her so long? Only her little sister could need the bathroom right as the opera was about to start. And as far as Emily could tell, the toilets in the ancient arena were few and far between and had queues centuries long. Meanwhile her mouth was dry and she wanted the six-foot-plus pillar blocking her view of centre stage to move. And then he did, turning right round as he held the gadget up in front of him. The flash of his grin was more blinding than the sudden flash of bright light.

'What—' she asked tartly '—you're taking photos now?'

'Sì.' He nodded, smiling like the Cheshire cat. 'I need a new wallpaper photo for my phone. And this is such a spectacular view, don't you think?'

'I think the "view" is *behind* you. You know, the stage, the set, the orchestra.'

'Oh, no, you're wrong. The beauty of the night is right in front of me.' As he put the phone thing in his pocket he held her gaze with a long, lazy, unmistakably challenging stare that she felt from the top of her head to her fingertips and all the way to her toes. And in all the secret spaces in between she burned. Spitting hot became unbearable— she was melting, literally melting at his feet. And stupidly she wished she were wearing something a little more glam than her cheap cotton skirt and tee combo. Why couldn't she have a gorgeous black gown, some serious bling and ice-queen sophistication to set it off?

She choked for real then—half giggling, half spluttering on a speck of something in her throat.

Eyes watering, she heard his call to the passing waiter. He spoke rapidly in Italian. She didn't catch a word of it. Only glimpsed the smile pass between the two men and then the money. He took the step separating where he stood and she sat, and handed her the bottle of water he'd just bought.

'For your throat.' Dry amusement was all obvious and all aggravating. 'Please.' He held the bottle a little closer, right in her face, and she knew he wasn't going to remove it.

What could she do? Act the totally irritated diva? She couldn't, not when the opera hadn't actually started, and he'd put the phone away and was suddenly smiling. It was some smile.

'Thank you,' she said, mentally blaming the breathiness of her reply on the awkward angle of her neck as she craned it right back to look at him.

He sat in the gap next to her. 'You're looking forward to the opera?'

'Yes.' Where was Kate? Where was the conductor? But time was playing tricks and the tiniest of moments became eons.

He nodded. 'It is a good one. They perform it every year here.'

'I know.' She'd read it in the tourist books she'd devoured from the library. Right now her eyes were devouring something else. Up close he wasn't just good-looking, he was incredible-looking. While his physical presence had been noticeable from a distance, nearer it was his expression that arrested her attention.

He was tall, he was dark, he was handsome. So far, so cliché. Like almost every man she'd seen in this city he was immaculately groomed. But there was so much more. There was the strong, angled jaw and the faint shadow of stubble. And in the heart of that was his mouth—wide and full—contrasting with the steep planes of his cheekbones. That mouth raised questions that Emily wanted to answer—was it as smooth as it looked? Warm or cool? It was certainly infinitely touchable. Utterly inviting.

Vying for first place with his lips were his eyes. Deep chocolate-brown, they were set off by the requisite thick, long lashes. But the chocolate didn't have the dull, matte quality of a solid block. It was warm and glossy and liquid, the dark variety—there was no diluting milky sweetness. And at the very centre there was a hardness—a 'don't go there' dangerous quality that totally aroused the curiosity of Pandora in Emily. It was like the bitterness at the bottom of a strong coffee or the darkest of dark chocolate that her taste buds both desired and recoiled from.

'Aren't you going to have your drink?' He didn't seem fazed by her scrutiny, instead seemed quite content to sit and study her right back. Closely.

She remembered the bottle and marvelled that steam wasn't rising from it. Surely the water should be boiling from the red-hot elements that were her hands?

'I think you should,' he spoke easily. 'You seem thirsty.'

That smile had broken the arrogant set to his features once more. A wide, sensual slash, his lips were surprisingly soft-looking, and framed white, straight, strong teeth. Oh, he had it all, didn't he? The height and body of a champion athlete, and the full features of a sensuous lover.

He glanced at the cheap cloth bag beside her, so obviously empty. 'You have no picnic? No lover to share the music and the magic of the night with you?' He gestured around them where many in the audience were snacking on treats stored in small baskets. Most were paired off, couples sitting close, the scent of romance heavy in the atmosphere.

'I'm here with my sister. She's just gone to get something.' Emily's defence mounted.

'Ah, your sister.' He nodded, tone cryptic.

For want of something, anything to stop her staring at him, she flipped the lid on the water bottle.

'Where are you from?'

It was obvious to him that she was foreign. He'd spoken in English to her from the off. She figured it was the travel garb, the ancient clothes that had left that budget chain store many seasons ago and hadn't ever seen an iron. She was no fabulous Italian fashionista.

'New Zealand.' She tossed her head, scraping for some pride.

A hint of surprise lifted his expression. 'You've come a long way. No wonder you're looking forward to the music.'

'Yes. I've wanted to come here for years.' It had been her fantasy escape. Now she wanted to know if Italy was as warm and flavoursome a country as she'd always imagined. The opera had been the way to convince Kate to stop here en route to London.

If Emily had both the choice and the money, she'd travel on to Venice, Florence, Rome…everywhere. Countless times she'd watched every Italian movie they had at the DVD store where she'd worked. She even had a few phrases to try out on friendly looking faces. She looked down at the stage, where the lights were gleaming and the orchestra was now waiting quietly. It was the realisation of a dream.

Her irritation melted away and she drank from the water bottle—a long, deep swig that ended with an unstoppable sigh of satisfaction.

Light, cool, strong fingers took her chin, and he turned her face back towards his. Stunned, she let him, silently absorbing the intensity of his expression, feeling it draw her even closer to him. And then it was only his index finger touching her, carefully sliding with gentle but firm pressure along her lower lip, rubbing the droplets of water into her dry lips.

'*Very* thirsty,' he said softly.

As his fingers caressed sensations surged within her— the sparks of bliss in her nerve endings, the devilish desire to flick out her tongue and taste him.

The audience of thousands was silent with expectation but it was nothing compared to the anticipation enthralling her. She didn't want him to break the delightful contact. Rather the wish for more rocketed. This was crazy. She couldn't want a complete stranger to kiss her, could she? To touch his lips to the spot where his finger now stroked?

But yes. Emily, who had never been one for flings, let

alone one-night stands, was almost overcome by the urge to lie back and let him do as he pleased—right here, right now, in an amphitheatre filled to capacity. The water bottle slid from her weak grasp to the stone seat beside her as she mumbled, 'You realise it's about to start?'

His gaze lowered, lids almost closing right over his eyes, hiding the sharpening gleam in the even darker chocolate. 'What makes you think it hasn't started already?'

Oh, my. His fingers left her mouth but brushed her thigh as he picked up the small candle that she'd completely forgotten. Instinctively every deep internal muscle within her tensed, wanted to squirm. The onward rush of sensation was heady and new and delightful. His eyes flipped back to hers, and she knew he was aware of the waves that were crashing over her, drowning her in unaccustomed, unexpected desire.

'Let's light this, *sì*?' He pulled a lighter from his pocket. There was a metallic click and the flicker sent a warm glow into his face. She couldn't look away—she was fascinated by the tension in his jaw, the firm curve of his mouth, the brilliance in his dark eyes. Inside and out, she adored his searing attention.

Luca made himself break free of her mesmerising stare and concentrated stupidly hard on lighting the candle. But when he held it out for her she didn't move and he just had to look close again. Like a statue she sat, still gazing at him with those sky-wide, sea-green eyes. He couldn't help grinning as he transferred the candle to his other hand, using his nearest to capture hers. God, she was gorgeous.

Honey-coloured hair and a softly curved figure in a pale green tee that brought out the depths in those eyes. He'd noticed her on his way up to get better reception for his phone and then he'd been entertained by her less than subtle methods of showing her displeasure at where he was standing. He'd strung out sending his text just to feel her reaction. And then he'd had to capture it—the sultry glare, the long legs bent beneath her.

Irresistible.

He felt her quiver, tightened his own fingers instinctively, and made her take the burning candle. For a nanosecond that felt like for ever, they held the flame together, his fist encompassing hers. He liked the feel of her in his hand. He'd like to feel more of her in his hand.

'You should have a lover to sit with at the opera.' If it were him he'd slide his arm around her and pull her in snug against his chest.

'So should you.' Her gaze was direct.

'True. Unfortunately I have other guests to entertain.' Helplessly he shrugged. 'But in a parallel universe I'd be here with you.'

'A total stranger?' Coy mockery flavoured her tone and her glance.

'We wouldn't be strangers for long.'

The green in her eyes deepened again and her mouth parted with the faintest of gasps. Yes, he did mean exactly that—they would be close and physical and fulfilled. And, yes, it was crazy. Since when did he sit holding the hand of a strange woman and fantasise about holding her in his arms? Since when did he think he could ever be fulfilled?

Not like that—not by connecting with another person. People—*relationships*—were beyond him. It was only from work that he sought satisfaction now.

Her colour steadily rose but still she held his gaze. 'What a shame there's no such thing as parallel universes.'

'Yes.' This fantasy was the strongest temptation—and he searched for a way to sustain it, just for a moment more. 'But there's always tomorrow.'

She smiled at that. 'Tomorrow.'

The burst of applause was deafening. He blinked and the bubble was burst. A quick glance down showed the conductor at the podium, his baton raised. He'd better get back to his seat—he did have guests to entertain. Damn. But he sent her a smile as he let go of her hand and stood. '*Ciao, bella.*'

CHAPTER TWO

EMILY spent the next moment of eternity trying to remember how to breathe. Then she shook her head and laughed weakly—puffing away the lingering intensity with a self-prescribed dose of sarcasm. What a flirt. He'd transformed her heat of anger into the heat of attraction, totally overcoming her annoyance and leaving her practically panting.

She watched as he descended the steps and re-entered the exclusive zone. He didn't look back. He'd already forgotten her. He must do it all the time—gaze at an unsuspecting female with his deep brown, dangerous eyes; lay a single finger on her person—of course she'd say yes in a heartbeat. No wonder he wore that mantle of lazy arrogance. He was the kind of guy for whom everything came easy—especially women.

But the surprising fact was, Emily would quite happily have been one of his women.

Irresistible.

As the opening chords of the overture began Kate flung into the cavernous space beside her.

'Great, you got some water,' she said, picking the bottle

up from beside Emily and half draining it. 'Just in time for the show.'

Emily pressed her finger on her needy lips—retracing the path his had taken. As far as she was concerned, the main event was already over.

But the Arena di Verona did not disappoint. Over two hours later as the applause thundered and cries of *encore* and *bravo* rang out, pleasure and relief rippled through Emily. It had been *so* worth it. The warmth, the atmosphere, the music, the spectacle—everything had been as wonderful as she could have wished. Well, almost everything. Somehow that fleeting encounter with a gorgeous stranger had made her miss something she hadn't had time to want until now—touch, pleasure, a sense of her own desirability. It had been a long time coming. She'd been too busy to date, and the one attempt at a boyfriend really hadn't been worth it. But suddenly, with one touch from him, that closed door to the sensual part of herself had been swung wide open. And now she was left wondering, wanting to walk through it.

She and Kate moved among the mass of bubbling, happy people, finding their way out of the amphitheatre and into the piazza where the crowd spilled and milled. Emily didn't want the night to end. She lingered, still feeling the vibrations from the sound of orchestra and voice, but most of all still feeling the touch of a finger on her lips…wanting *more*.

'Did you think the soprano was a bit off in that last duet?'

Emily knew Kate was about to dissect the performance note by note, but honestly she hadn't been listening too close in that one. She'd hadn't been able to stop her gaze from travelling down to a certain spot in the rich seats where a dark head was slightly elevated above the others. The music had become the soundtrack to the kind of fantasy that she didn't usually have time to indulge in.

'Umm, which bit?' Warmth pervaded her entire body and she smiled, reliving the secret pleasure of that chance meeting. Then she glanced at her sister, saw her mouth open and the deep breath. Her smile disappeared altogether as Kate launched full tilt into the final refrain of the biggest 'hit' of the night.

'Kate!' Emily whispered—mentally screaming. How embarrassing. But her sister just threw her a naughty glance and kept on going. As people turned to look a moat of space appeared around them and Emily longed for a lifeboat to take her back into the crowd. She scanned it, discomfort prickling as more and more turned their way. Then she saw the group of well-dressed men. He stood in the centre, half a head taller. Striking, and staring right in their direction. There was a woman there too. Of course there was. Standing right beside him—beautiful and elegant, obviously an Italian fashionista and obviously interested in him. A lover to sit with at the opera?

A stupidly strong sense of loss washed through her. They'd only shared a few words on the steps, but it had felt as if a myriad of possibilities had been unveiled. But she wasn't anything like the woman he was with, so there was no 'possibility' after all, and her disappointment was bitter.

The second Kate paused for breath Emily grasped her arm, propelling her forwards. 'Are you done?'

'No.' Kate threw a smile in the direction of anyone still looking their way and fell into step. 'I've had a great idea.'

Emily didn't want to listen. Emily just wanted to get away. But, unlike him, Emily had to look back. She turned her head over her shoulder for one final glimpse. He was staring right at her, smile curling upwards, and as she met his gaze he winked. She didn't smile, but she kept looking, needing to capture his image in her mind for one final moment before turning away.

They rounded the corner into one of the busy side streets and Kate lurched to a halt. 'I am not just having bread for the next two days. We're in Italy. I want pasta, I want pizza. I want a restaurant.'

'Kate.' Emily was close to exasperation point. Why couldn't she understand that they just didn't have the funds for that?

'I'm going to get us some more money.'

'How?'

'Busking.'

'Kate.' Emily's heart sank. She knew what her sister was like—the attention she'd got would only have whetted her appetite.

'Come on, Em, you saw the crowd that gathered just then. Three songs and we'll have enough for the most fabulous meal tomorrow—one of those long, lazy lunches at one of those tables outside, with millions of courses and lots of wine.'

Admittedly Emily's mouth was watering at the idea but she tried to ignore it. 'You're probably supposed to have permits to perform.'

Kate yawned big and fake. 'Rules, Em?'

'One of us has to be responsible.' And she always had been—as a matter of necessity. She'd had sole responsibility for the two of them for years. Mother, father, sister, friend, breadwinner, cook, cleaner, chauffeur—all rolled into one.

'It's a shame there's no piano for you to accompany me. Unless you want to do that duet?'

'Not on your life.' Kate could have the limelight. Emily was happy to accompany but centre stage was too bright for her.

'I'll only be ten minutes. No one will mind.'

Emily sighed and stepped to the side, watching as Kate shook out her hair from under her straw hat. Her sister was impetuous, impulsive and impossible to say no to and, as she'd predicted, she had a crowd around her within minutes. Emily wasn't surprised. With her long red locks and slender figure, Kate turned heads even before she opened her mouth. And when she started singing? The angelic, pure tones made anything with ears stop and listen. As the crowd of people thickened Kate flung her a triumphant glance and truly got into her stride. Emily stood to the side and looked around, anxiously keeping an eye for sight of a *carabiniere*, not wanting to get into trouble.

'Your sister is talented.'

She jumped. He was right behind her. She turned a fraction, and yes, really, he was there—looming large. Her body went hypersensitive. Her brain threatened to shut down altogether. 'Yes.'

'And so are you.'

Umm, how did he figure that? She shook her head. 'Not quite in the same way.'

'No,' he agreed before his voice dropped, the alien lilt becoming more audible. 'Your sister is still a child. Whereas you, I think, have the talents of a woman.'

Emily drew a sharp breath and turned to face him full on. 'You've got to be kidding.'

'No.' His dark eyes held hers, amused and challenging. 'You send me a look like that over your shoulder? What choice did I have but to follow?'

The gauntlet had been thrown. Silver fire raced through her veins. She had the talents of a woman? If only she did—why, then she'd have him on his knees before her, with all his arrogance and experience rendered useless. Wanting her beyond reason and willing to grant her anything—the crazy idea sent a thrill through her. Since when was she any kind of sex goddess? When was it that she'd last *had* sex?

She forgot about Kate warbling in the background, forgot about the woman she'd seen near him, only heard the humour in his voice, only saw the sexy smile… To be talking suggestively like this was so foreign, but so much fun. She wanted it to continue.

She tried an almost saucy reply. 'If that's the case, then perhaps you should be careful.'

His smile went wicked. 'Definitely.' He held out his hand. 'Luca Bianchi.'

She glanced to his hand and then back to his face, letting her own smile go sinful. 'You're not afraid I might bite?'

'I'm half hoping you will.'

She lifted her hand. 'Emily Dodds.' The frisson raced up her arm as contact was made.

'Emily.' The way he said it made her toes and everything inside her curl up tight. His hand gripped hers firmly. 'Did you enjoy the opera?'

'I loved it.'

He nodded. 'It was a good performance.'

'And a lovely atmosphere.'

'My company could have been a little better. How about yours?'

'It wasn't bad.'

'But it could have been better.'

'Perhaps.' Faux demurely, she looked down. 'Are you going to give me my hand back?'

'I was thinking I might keep it and take it home with me.'

'Not tonight.' She refused, but she couldn't hold back her smile. Pleasure thrilled through her—to be so overtly admired, courted, frankly *chased*…by a man as attractive as this was heady stuff.

'No? What a shame.' His mouth curved too. 'But there's always tomorrow.'

For a long moment she stared into his melting chocolate eyes, a million 'if onlys' circulating in her head. His fingers tightened.

'See, I told you!' Kate bubbled up, shaking her upturned hat in front of her. 'Enough for a five-course feast in a fancy restaurant.'

Emily tugged her hand and after a gentle squeeze he let it slip from his.

'Singing for your supper?' he asked dryly.

'Lunch tomorrow!' Kate answered. 'Hi, I'm Kate.'

'Hello, Kate. I'm Luca. I'm a friend of your sister's.'

Emily glanced at him. *Friend?* There was a tease in his eyes directed totally at her. 'Let me get you two a drink. You must be thirsty after performing in the heat like this.'

'Oh, we—' The sensible side of Emily thought she should refuse. But there was a whisker of a wink again. It was enough to tip her over. She was in Italy—her dream holiday destination—and she was flirting with the dreamiest guy imaginable. Little Miss Sassy elbowed Little Miss Sensible out of the way for good. 'Thanks.'

Luca tried and failed to remember when he'd ever done anything as crazy as this. It had been so long, yet all of a sudden he was chasing hard for something that could only be momentary. But, hell, it would be fun. And wasn't he due for a little fun? While the waiter fetched the wine, Luca tried to remind himself that in reality one-night stands were never as good as you thought they were going to be, but gave up after half a thought. Fact was, he hadn't wanted a woman quite like this, quite in this way, ever. An instant, visceral demand—his whole body was tight with anticipation.

It was going to happen; he'd make certain of it. Therefore he didn't need to be staring at her like some starving dog. However, controlling that urge was something of a problem when she looked at him like that—green eyes glittering with both challenge and caution.

'What brings you to Verona?' He made small but necessary talk.

'We're on our way to London,' the sister answered. 'I want to sing there.'

He spared a quick glance for the pretty young redhead and her pale blue eyes. She could do it if she wanted. 'You have the talent to sing anywhere. But do you have the determination?'

'Absolutely.'

His gaze was drawn back to the other direction—Emily. Scattered across her nose were a few freckles that he'd like to kiss and beneath that a mouth that he wanted to kiss even more. She didn't have the girlish skinny physique of her sister. She'd still be considered trim but with more curves and length. Hips to cushion his, legs to wrap around his waist, hair to wind round his wrist and tug on so he could access her neck and kiss his way down to her full breasts.

As Kate babbled on about her career plans he sipped his wine and watched the faint dusky pink blush spread over Emily's face. The more he watched, the more it spread and the deeper the colour grew. His own temperature began to lift.

'You want a wonderful lunch, Kate?' He finally interrupted the incessant flow. 'I know just the place. You and Emily meet me outside here tomorrow at one and I'll take you.'

'Really?' Kate's desire was too easy to please. He had the suspicion her sister might be more of a challenge—but a very welcome one.

'Absolutely. It would be my pleasure.' He directed that last word right to Emily, allowing in the faint provocation. All the pleasure would be in seeing her.

She lifted her gaze from her seemingly minute contemplation of her empty glass. Her eyes were such a deep green—thoughtful, assessing, seeking. He met them squarely. If they were alone it would be so easy. But they weren't alone—not yet—and he had to hold back from moving the way he wanted. So for the first time in his life he found himself almost begging. 'It'll be the best you've ever had.'

'Tomorrow?' It was the kid sister all excited.

'Yes.' He refused to break the bond with Emily, only vaguely satisfied when he saw the faint upward tweak of her lips. 'Tomorrow.'

When Emily walked to the piazza with Kate, they found Luca waiting, as promised, in front of the Arena. But he was not alone. On either side of him stood a beautiful woman. A cold, hard ball grew in Emily, freezing her throat, her chest, her tummy. What was he doing—building a harem? And yet as she walked towards him his eyes seemed to be eating her up. When his long, intense stare finally made it up to her face she was all hot again. Desire, curiosity, a wanting for a kind of wickedness—and above all vexation about those two other women. What made it worse was that she knew he'd read her expression, and right now he looked totally smug.

When they got within earshot it was to Kate that he turned. 'Kate, meet Maria and Anne—both singers with the opera of the Arena di Verona. How would you like to spend the afternoon touring backstage and join in a rehearsal?'

Kate's eyes were shining. 'Really?'

Luca laughed, indulgence audible. 'Yes, really. But wait, there's more.' His tone was full of irony. He handed

her an envelope. 'I have a contact that you might find use-
ful in London. Here are the details. Be sure to get in touch
because he's expecting to hear from you.'

'Really?' Kate's shriek was right up there at the top of
her vocal range.

'Maria and Anne will ensure you get some lunch. Perhaps
not five courses in a fancy restaurant, but something.'

'Oh, it doesn't matter. I'm not that hungry anyway.'

'Fine, so run along, then. These two will take care of
you.'

And she was just like a child, thrilled to have had her most
prized wish granted. Not even sparing Emily a second glance.

'Kate, will you be—?' Emily didn't get the 'OK' out.

'Em, don't be a nag. I'm nearly nineteen, remember?
Back home I can drink, drive and vote.'

'Yeah, but not all in the same afternoon.' Officially she
might be all grown up but Emily couldn't seem to shake
the responsibility just yet. Kate was all she had.

But her sister was practically skipping, already asking
question after question of the two professional singers.

'Don't worry, Kate,' Luca drawled after her. 'I'll take
care of Emily.'

Kate didn't turn, simply sang back, 'I know.'

Emily watched them depart, not trusting herself to meet
his gaze too soon. He'd take care of her? At twenty-four
she didn't need taking care of, but she had the feeling he
didn't mean in the protective parental sense.

After a long silent moment he spoke—quietly but, oh,
so clearly. 'So, Emily, it's just you and me.'

She inclined her head, silently applauding him. This

was a man who would get what he wanted—every time. And in that moment she knew that if she was what he wanted, she was what he would get.

She was free. Her sister—her responsibility—was gone for the afternoon, she was on holiday in the most beautiful city and she wanted to explore *everything*.

'I said I'd show you the best of Verona. Are you willing?'

She looked at him then. Raised a single eyebrow so they both knew she was. His broad smile made one of its appearances—boyish and fun and infectious. 'Then let's walk.'

She couldn't hold back the answering smile, nor could she quell the shiver as he took her hand. His grip tightened and he flashed a whisker of a wink, before leading them towards a side street.

'Where are you taking me?'

'On a brief tour of some of the city's highlights and then to lunch. Sound OK?'

'Sounds fine.'

He stopped. 'Don't swamp me with your enthusiasm, Emily.'

'No, that sounds great.'

'Have you seen Casa de Giulietta?'

'Yes.' Supposedly Juliet's balcony from Romeo and Juliet—aside from the fact that that story was fiction.

'Of course you have. Did you leave a message?'

'No.' People left love notes and prayers on the wall.

'No lover to leave a message for?'

How many times was he going to ask her that one? 'Actually I'm not a fan of graffiti.' She sidestepped with a grin and then narrowed her gaze at him. 'Have you ever left a message there?'

'I'm not romantic. What about Castelvecchio and San Zeno—been to those?'

'Yes.'

'Duomo?'

'Yes.'

He frowned and stopped walking. 'How long have you been in Verona?'

'This is our fifth day. For the first two I took Kate on a route march around the city. I think I've seen most of the essentials.'

'So that wasn't your first opera at the Arena? They perform every other night.'

'I know, but it was. We couldn't afford to go twice. I just wanted to spend some time in Italy.'

'Did you manage a day trip to Venice?'

'Yes.' She beamed. 'It was wonderful.'

'Right.' He pulled on her hand and started walking quickly in the opposite direction from which they'd started.

'Where are we going now?'

'Straight to lunch.'

Excellent. Emily's feeling of freedom grew as he led her across a bridge to the other side of the river and along a little farther until they reached some gates. Turning to her, his eyes sparkling with irresistibly sinful promise, he invited, 'Come into the Giardino with me, Emily.'

CHAPTER THREE

GIARDINO GIUSTI. The beautiful Renaissance gardens had been designed centuries ago and were magnificent. The green upon green of the trees was a pleasant contrast to the grey and stone of the buildings in the centre of town. They wound their way through the formal topiary section. And although it was quieter and should have been cooler, all Emily felt was hotter and more attuned to the tiniest of sounds—the trickle of water, the hum of a bee, the shortness of her own breath…and the nearness of him.

He led her along a path, to where it seemed to be a little wilder, more shade, taller trees and a moist grotto not far in the distance. She looked at a shaded grassy bank.

'Oh, look, someone's having a picnic.'

'Yes.' He smiled that boyish smile. 'We are.'

He walked up to the dark-suited man standing beside the spread. They spoke briefly and then the man walked away, down the path to the exit.

Luca gestured for her to come closer. 'You're hungry?'

As she stared she felt her insides light up. 'And you say

you're not romantic, Luca?' she gently mocked to cover the thrill.

'It's a simple picnic.'

There was nothing simple about it. A large, ruby-red blanket was spread, and scattered on top of it were round cushions in heavy, gilt fabric—deeper reds, threaded with gold. Another rug was folded on one corner—what, should they need more room or was it for them to hide beneath? Oh, Emily was tickled…and so tempted.

Beside the space upon which they were so clearly meant to recline stood a large basket. Luca had knelt beside it already and pulled out wine. As he poured into the crystal glasses Emily decided she'd entered paradise.

Unhesitatingly she sat on the rug, accepted the glass he gave her and looked across the view of the impeccably maintained garden, needing a moment to recapture her sanity before she tossed all caution aside.

'This is incredible.'

'The best of Italy.' He smiled, as if he knew she'd already lost it. 'Here for you.'

'The basket doesn't look big enough.'

'I wasn't referring to the basket.'

'Very sure of your own worth, aren't you?'

'Down to the last euro, yes. But we're not talking money now.'

'No?'

'We're talking pleasure. And you can't put a price on absolute pleasure.'

* * *

Luca couldn't look away from her. Her expression of delight was so genuine, so pleased, it made him feel guilty 'I didn't pick all this, or lay it out.'

She laughed. 'I know. But it was your idea.'

It was. And now he felt even more guilty—he wanted to wine, dine and woo her. For one night only. And for all her fiery eyes and flirting she was more sweet than sophisticated. Really, he had no right to mess with her, not unless she wanted it too. Not unless she understood the rules. A one-off, holiday fling. 'The hotel prepared the food.'

'So I get the five-course feast.'

'You do.'

'How come you have connections at the opera?'

'My company is a corporate sponsor.'

'Your company?'

'*Mine.*' It was all his and it was all his life. He had spent almost the entire decade dedicated to it. Getting his education, the experience and growing the private finance firm into the extreme success it was. He had taken no help from his father. He didn't need his uninterested parent throwing him nothing but pretty patterned paper. He could make his own money, prove his own worth. 'I often take valued clients and their wives.'

'Their wives?'

'*Sì.*' He suppressed a smile. So she'd wondered about the woman with them last night. Yes, she was the wife of a client and, no, he wasn't interested. He sent her a meaningful look, but saw she was checking out his left hand. He tensed. He'd worn a ring on that finger once. He'd kept it on for some time after—using it like a talisman to ward off

women. But every time he'd looked at it he'd been reminded. Nikki hadn't had the strength to push it on and
he'd had to do it himself. And despite its tiny circumfer-
ence, the ring he'd given her had hung loose, threatening
to slide over her bony knuckle. There hadn't been an engagement ring. There hadn't been time.

Eventually he'd taken his ring off and allowed the sun
to brown the pale mark. But even so he couldn't forget.
Even now, when he was plotting a moment of madness, the
memory clung to him, reminding him of what not to do:
don't ever get attached.

'What does your company do?'

'Hedge funds.' Good, when painful thoughts impinged
he turned back to work—that was the way Luca liked it.

'Hedges?' Her nose wrinkled. 'So it's like gardens?'

He hesitated, unwilling to launch into a detailed expla-
nation of the complex transactions he managed, so he
fudged it instead. 'I like making things grow.'

'Money trees.' Her eyes were sparkling with amusement.

He laughed—her naiveté had been a ploy and she was
teasing him. 'Right.'

'And you like the opera?'

Why did she think that was a surprise? 'I'm Italian, of
course I like the opera.'

'You don't sound all that Italian.'

'The curse of my education—boarding school in
England from the age of seven. Over a decade 'til I
emerged from the system. But I guess I inherited my ap-
preciation of the opera from my mother.' But more painful
memories lurked with the mention of her so he moved the

conversation back to Emily. 'Do you like Italy?' He didn'
need to hear her answer, already had it as her face lit up
and it was his turn to tease. 'Your first visit, right? Is it everything you hoped it would be?'

'Actually it's better.'

There was that genuine, warm enthusiasm again. Her
anger had risen from that last night—based on the desire
to enjoy herself, to make the most of the moment she'd obviously been waiting a while for. The freshness was tan-
talising. 'Are you enjoying the food?'

She nodded.

'Have you tried some of the local specialities?'

She looked vague so perhaps not. Of course, budget
was an issue. He could help out with that today. 'Italian
cuisine isn't just buffalo mozzarella and sun-dried tomatoes, you know.'

'No?' She pouted. 'But I love buffalo mozzarella and
sun-dried tomatoes.'

He chuckled. 'Come on, try some more with me now.'

He delved deeper into the basket. The hotel had done a
fabulous job, filling it with many small containers, each
holding samples of this and that. Some were simple, just a
few olives, other were complex miniatures of great dishes.

He lifted them out and explained them to her, where each
came from, made her say the Italian name for them and then
watched as she tried each, waiting for her reaction before
tasting them himself. And all the while, his appetite grew.

Emily licked the sweet oil from her lips. Yes, she loved
sun-dried tomatoes but, my goodness, the nibbles in those

containers were out of this world. By now, eating as much as she had, under the shade of the trees, in this warmth, she would ordinarily have been overcome with laziness. But his presence, so close, precluded that. He was stretched out, propped up on one elbow, his long, athletic length stretching from one end of the blankets to the other. Relaxed.

Emily ached to touch him now—one appetite filled, another starving. Instead she took a breadstick from the box, needing something to fiddle with.

'Tell me about your life.' He looked across the small gap between them now littered with lids and containers, to where she sat up, legs curled beneath her.

She wrinkled her nose. 'There's really not that much to tell.' There really wasn't, certainly nothing glamorous or exciting.

'Where are your parents?'

As she broke the grissini in two the shadow on her heart must have crossed her face.

'I'm sorry,' he said quietly. 'Will you tell me what happened?'

'Of course.' She smiled the moment away. 'It was a long time ago.' She broke one half of the grissini into quarters and gave him the potted summary. 'Mum died in a car crash when I was fifteen. After the accident Dad went into a decline. He drank a lot. Smoked. Stopped eating.' She rubbed the crumbs between her fingers and looked down at the trees. 'I think with her gone he lost the will to live.'

'Even though he had two beautiful daughters to look after?'

She could understand the question, perceived the faint

judgment. Hadn't she thought the same in those moments of anger that had sometimes come in the wee small hours? But she also knew the whole story; things never were black and white—shades of grey all the way. And so she shared a part of it.

'He was driving the car, Luca. He never got over the guilt.' She flicked away the final crumb, sat back on her hands and stared down the gentle slope to the row of cypresses. 'He died two years after her.'

Two years of trying to get him through it. But the depression had pulled him so far down and the drinking had gone from problem to illness and the damage to his mind and body had become irreparable. He couldn't climb out of it and he didn't want to. He simply shut down. Emily had taken over everything.

'What happened then?'

'I was eighteen. Kate was nearly thirteen. They let her stay with me. I left school and got a job.'

Emily had been thinking of studying piano at university but instead she'd worked and they'd put all they had into Kate's singing. Her younger sister had the looks, the talent and the drive. Now, nearly nineteen, she was determined to come overseas and make her break before, as she put it, she got 'over the hill'. Emily was her accompanist—both in terms of playing the piano for her to sing, and in terms of support.

'So you looked after Kate.'

Emily shrugged. 'We looked after each other.' There was no one else.

The silence was long and finally she looked at him. The

darkness in his eyes reflected the dark days. Somehow he knew. He understood the struggle and the loneliness. And for a second there she thought she saw pity. Well, she didn't want that—not today, not from him. She'd lived through it, she'd survived and so had Kate. Now they were off, heading towards that new horizon. Life was moving forward. And she was totally trying to ignore the fear thumping in the pit of her stomach. For the last six years she'd worked two jobs plus done all the household chores. She'd created stability, routine…now nothing was stable, there was no routine and she couldn't foresee the future. All she knew was that she wanted more than what her life had been back home. A more satisfying job, a more satis-fying social life… And sitting with this gorgeous man in this beautiful garden, it felt as if the chance to open up a new part of her life was being offered right now.

'What about you?' she asked, lightening her tone. 'Where's your family?'

His face tightened and she knew the shadow was a match for her own. 'Really?'

'Cancer killed my mother when I was seven.' He spoke bluntly but it was clear the pain was still sharp.

'And your father?'

He shrugged. 'I went to boarding school straight after. We're not close.' The bare recitation spoke volumes.

She sat back, shocked. He'd been sent away? To a whole other country where they didn't even speak his first lan-guage?

The slight smile in his eyes was all cynical. 'I take after my mother. I think I was too painful a reminder.'

So in a way they'd both been rejected by their surviving parent. Luca had been sent away, and Emily's father had gone away himself—in mind and spirit anyway—leaving Emily to shoulder the burden of caring for his fading shell.

'Where's your dad now?'

'He remarried. They live just outside Rome.'

Their eyes met. Was that part of what had drawn them together? That somehow they'd recognised that they had shadows in common?

She barely had the chance to process that when he sat up. 'Enough gloom. The day is too short.' He reached into the apparently bottomless basket. 'Let's try dessert.'

Perhaps their pasts had nothing to do with the attraction. Perhaps it all came down to the fact that he was the most physically dynamic man she'd ever seen. And he was right. They didn't need to share more in the way of gloom. Today was about holidays and sun.

The dessert was some creamy confection. He held the spoon, his laughter a soft rumble as he made her lean closer to taste it.

Oh, my. It was the taste of pure decadence.

'Good, isn't it?' He had a spoonful and then offered her another.

'Mmm-hmm.'

She stretched out and lay back on the pillow then, giving herself over to the utter indulgence. Closing her eyes, letting her mind savour the flavour and soak up the heat. She wanted more of the sweet, wanted much more of him.

'So all this time you've been looking after your sister,'

he spoke softly. 'Now you need someone to satisfy *your* needs.'

She turned her head and opened her eyes. His head was close, resting on the cushion right by hers. 'What makes you think I haven't got someone already?'

'If you did, you wouldn't be looking at me with those hungry eyes.'

She lifted her head, a little on her dignity. 'You don't need to lay it on with a trowel, Luca. I'm not completely inexperienced.'

'Only *relatively*, *sì*?' He laughed. 'What was he? Some young fool who wouldn't know how to give pleasure to a woman even if she gave him step by step instructions and a map showing the way?'

She felt the blush covering her cheeks and neck and she shut her eyes again to pretend it wasn't happening. Her ex had been exactly like that.

'Emily. I can offer you nothing but a memory.' His voice was a little strained. 'But I think it would be some memory.'

She reopened her eyes then—drawn by the power behind his words.

'When did you last do something *you* wanted to do?' he asked. 'Not something for someone else, or something you *had* to do. But something you wanted, just for you?'

She couldn't remember. And she knew he knew. 'Is that what you're offering? How generous of you, Luca,' she mocked gently. 'As if there's nothing in it for you.'

'There's everything in it for me. I admit it.' He shrugged. 'I'm selfish. Be selfish with me.' He raised himself back up on one elbow, rolling onto his side to face her. 'We have more in common than you might think. I've been working hard too and you've worked hard for so long. Don't you deserve a treat?'

'Is that what you are?'

He leaned closer. 'You tell me.' He reached across and took her hand, lifted it and pressed it to his chest. 'Feel it? Accelerating?'

The solid thump in his chest was strong and regular and hypnotic and her fingers wanted the fabric to disappear so she could feel his skin direct.

'Is it like this for you, when we touch? When our arms brush as we walk side by side, does your body want more? Mine does.' He still spoke quietly but she felt the force of his underlying feeling pierce through to her marrow. 'What if I did that to you, Emily—would your heart start to race?'

It already was—faster and faster with every word and the spiralling anticipation.

'I think we should find out.' He let her hand go and reached across to her, his fingers drawing along the line of her collarbone.

'Luca…' She shook her head but couldn't deny the fire his touch ignited.

His hand slid down, pressed against her tee shirt, pulling it close to her skin, so that her breast was displayed, and he looked at her tight, peaking nipple. He smiled as it jutted out for him; he didn't need to feel her heart to know his effect on her.

He looked back into her face, intensely determined. 'Just one kiss.'

One afternoon. One absolute temptation.

He didn't need to coax her mouth open. She met him halfway, already wet and pliant and seeking. She closed her eyes, able to focus on nothing but him. And there was nothing but his kiss. His mouth moved over hers, his tongue probing, tasting. Rapidly it became more insistent—plundering, taking. She raised her hands, sliding them into his hair. Surrendering and then beginning to make her own demands—opening wider, seeking deeper, harder.

It was bliss. She wanted it to last, wanted to savour each stage. But too soon she wanted more. The need to move closer grew, she wanted him to roll right above her, wanted to feel his weight, to be pressed down into the soft rugs by his hard hips, wanted to explore his...

He drew back. 'Emily.'

She opened her eyes, hating the interruption.

'I am going to take you back to my hotel and kiss you like that all over your body. Is that OK with you?'

'Is your hotel far?'

He laughed, an uncontrolled shout of genuine amusement.

'I'm serious. Can't we just do this some more here?' She didn't want to wait. She wanted it all, right now.

He smiled, that wonderful warm, relaxed smile, and leaned over her again. The kiss was right back at hot. And then he was kissing her jaw, her throat, his hand was at her breast and she learnt him too, learning the boundaries with her touch—learning that with Luca there *were* no boundaries. The kisses and caresses were so intense and satisfying yet awakening such an appetite that she knew there would be no saying no. No tomorrow and no regrets. There was only now and a need so great it was overwhelming.

Through heavy eyes she saw the blue of the sky and the green of the branches above them, felt the heat of summer, and all her senses appreciated this paradise. And there was more to come; he promised so much more with every kiss. She shifted on the rug, restless. She'd never known how desire could be a sort of suffering, hadn't felt this depth of longing for physical fulfilment. The pain of it and the way the body could absolutely overrule reason.

He groaned, as if he too were in pain, and as if he'd read her mind and knew how willing she was, how much she wanted. 'I'd love to see you naked under these trees, but the Giardino is public. Unless spending the night with the *carabinieri* is on your list of tourist activities, then we need to leave. Now.'

She almost, almost didn't care, caught between not wanting this moment to end and wanting to get to the end as fast as possible—to completion.

'OK.' She forced the answer; it was like dragging herself out of the warmest, sweetest water. And all she wanted to do was disappear into the depths again. Had he drugged her with that food? But, no, it was his body, and his touch, that were the opiate.

He rose to his feet and held out his hand. 'Then come.'

Their eyes met for a pregnant moment. And then she smiled.

'What about this?' She gestured to the rumpled rug and scattered cushions and containers, not wanting to have to

think about them, but years of taking responsibility insisted
on it.

He shook his head. 'It's taken care of. Don't worry.'

He took her hand and led her down the sloping gardens.
Waiting at the gates was a sleek grey car. Luca held the
door open for her and she slid in. He climbed in the back
with her. The driver pulled away. It was only minutes to
the centre of Verona and his hotel, but all of them were
occupied as with light fingers he turned her head towards
him and kissed her. She didn't want to stop. She didn't want
him ever to stop.

CHAPTER FOUR

SURFACING from the car into a hazy reality, Emily walked beside Luca into the hotel. When she finally focused on her surroundings she almost stumbled. Opulence wasn't the word. And suddenly she feared she had no place here in her crumpled skirt and camping tee shirt. It was the early afternoon and they were walking into his hotel for an erotic indulgence. She was so turned on, she could hardly walk for the way she'd gone weak at the knees, and she had the horrible feeling that everyone must know. It was so strong to her that surely it must be obvious to everyone else? She longed to return to the quiet solitude they'd had in the warm gardens. This was sophisticated and exclusive and so not her.

He seemed to sense her discomfort, taking her arm and shielding her from the eyes of those in Reception. Smoothly he guided her through the lobby to the lift. It wasn't a possessive touch, he didn't put his arm around her and haul her close, it was merely a light hand at her elbow, and the simplicity and the politeness made the doubts wane. There was respect in his manner and she knew he had every intention of taking care of her. Suddenly nothing else mattered.

He didn't maul her in the lift either, stood beside her quietly, keeping his hand still light on her arm as he escorted her onto his floor. He swiped the key card and opened the door. She walked in, relieved to be alone with him again but still knocked sideways. He didn't just have a room, he had a suite. She'd guessed he had money, understood he was a financier of some sort. But she hadn't realised it was quite like this.

She turned to study him, reassessing. All Italians dressed nicely, didn't they?

'Second thoughts?' He was watching her just as keenly. 'It's OK to say no.'

Concentrating on him made the intimidating surroundings disappear. She melted all over again.

'No,' she said, then smiled naughtily at the flash in his eyes. 'I don't want to say no,' she elaborated firmly.

She watched, quite pleased as with obvious effort he unclenched his jaw. 'Good.'

'It will be the best, won't it, Luca?' She searched for final reassurance. Having had a sample of what could only be heaven, she didn't want disappointment. She'd had that before. 'I want the best.' And she did. To be lost from herself for just a few magic moments. One afternoon where she could forget the past and ignore the future. Let go of worries and responsibilities and be free to feel pleasure. It would be the first time and she'd been waiting for ever.

He closed the gap between them with slow, sure steps.

His finger traced her lower lip as it had the night at the opera. 'Don't doubt it.'

Her eyelids lowered slowly as the crazy lethargy returned. It was as if her senses were tuning out everything except him—his touch, his voice, his scent and his determination. There would be no saying no. It wasn't even an option, not for her.

This magic, this mysterious man—she wanted to know no more, except of his body. It had been there, from the first glance, the blink and reassessment that had happened in the quickest instance—one body's recognition of the other.

She didn't believe in love at first sight. But now she most certainly believed in lust at first sight. Her body programmed to seek his as her mate. It had never happened to her before. The few dates she'd been on, that past boyfriend—she'd felt nothing. But this, this was as if she'd been branded with a white-hot iron—*his*.

She hadn't been able to take her eyes off him. She still couldn't. Through her half-closed lids she watched him concentrate as slowly, so slowly, the tips of his fingers moved from her lips, brushing down her jaw, her neck and down the slope of her chest. She went taut with anticipation but his path diverted, going around her nipples rather than directly over them. She hissed out her breath, wanting him to touch her there.

But his fingers skimmed down her sides, and then took the hem of her tee shirt. Carefully he raised it, automatically she lifted her arms to help. In a second he had it off her, and tossed it to the side.

She stared at him, unashamed about the way her full breasts were trying to burst out of her bra, at the way her nipples were pressing hard against the fabric—begging him the only way they could. She just wanted him to *touch*.

His jaw was clenched hard again. His hands lifted. The light, gentle fingertips went back to her waist, slipping around her skirt to find the zip.

She wriggled her hips to help it slide down. And then she was standing before him, for a second stupidly hoping that it didn't matter that her bra and briefs didn't match.

He curved his arms right around her, fingers at work once more, unclasping the hooks. The straps loosened. He tweaked them at her shoulder and the shells of her bra slipped from her breasts.

For a moment there was nothing, only his fierce attention as he looked, colour rising in his face. She was almost about to plead when his hands lifted, cupping her breasts the way her bra had, only pushing them a little higher and then closer together. His thumbs rubbed gently over her peaking nipples as his hands explored their soft weight.

Her mouth opened, unconsciously doing what she wanted him to do—to open up and taste her.

His gaze lifted to meet hers, reading her expression, revealing his own hot desire. And then his mouth caught hers in a kiss that was deep and carnal and demanding, his tongue driving in and claiming. She met him, stroke for stroke, thrusting her hands into his hair and holding him. But he moved his kiss. Following the path his fingers had taken from her mouth, her jaw, her neck until finally, thankfully he was kissing her chest, up the slopes to where his hands held her breasts, pushing them together so his tongue could assault both her nipples with strong licks, and then he sucked her into his mouth.

She swayed towards him, the heat turning mass and muscle to liquid. But at her unbridled moan he lifted away, his thumbs instantly working to soothe the yearning in her breasts.

'Do you want me to take my shirt off, or do you want to do it yourself?' His breathlessness heightened her longing.

She too was breathing hard but she couldn't pass on the challenge or the pleasure. 'Let me.'

She fumbled with the first button but got the knack of them after the next. Drinking in the sight of his chest as it was slowly revealed. She reached out a hand, touched the hard heat of it, feeling the roughness where hair dappled it, finally placing her hand back over his heart. To where he'd placed it in the garden but this time on bare skin, feeling the life force beating, feeling the rhythm. And then she scraped his nipple with the tip of her thumb, watched the definition of his abs go even sharper. She pushed the shirt off his broad shoulders, stretching her arms wide to reach down his arms. All rock-hard, barely restrained muscle.

At that she didn't hesitate to go lower and pull out the loop of his belt. His trousers dropped to the floor. Then she was confronted with his boxers—and their package.

She blew out the breath she'd seemed to be holding for ever. Feeling the heat suffuse her cheeks, she tried to stretch the fabric over his large erection. Until, hands shaking, feeling both embarrassed and excited, she mumbled, 'I think you better do…that bit.'

He caught her wrists and pulled her close, laughter rumbling in his chest. 'But shouldn't that be the best bit?'

She nodded. 'I'm sure it is, but I might need a moment to get used to it.'

He kissed her again, long and deep, and then without warning pushed her back onto the bed, coming down hard on top. She wriggled, unbelievably happy to have the weight of him on her at last.

He held his head from hers, teasing. 'I think we should take things very, very slow.'

If this was taking things slow, then heaven help her if he decided to speed them up.

But then he did go slow. Kisses trailed and fingers toyed as he did as he'd promised and kissed her all over her body. As he peeled off her panties and made his way back to the tops of her thighs she couldn't hold back the squirm—overly aware of what was going to happen.

'Don't be shy,' he said calmly.

She breathed in deep. He was right. Why be shy? This was her afternoon, after all. She reached out a hand, felt the strength of his thigh. Rubbed her fingers through the masculine hair, felt the muscles working underneath it. And found her appetite to explore more was ravenous. How good he felt beneath her fingers—how much better might he feel beneath her lips? So she tried exactly that. Never had she had such a body to explore before—to taste, to delight in. Now she understood why humans sought beauty, marvelled in it, celebrated it.

Perfection.

Silently he let her play, she could feel him watching her,

feel the tension mounting until he suddenly jerked away from her, pulling open the drawer in the table beside the bed so hard the whole thing fell out. No matter, he had what he wanted, was out of the boxers, had rolled the condom on and she watched and smiled, knowing that soon, soon, soon, she would have all that *she* wanted.

He took the lead again, pinning her down with his heavy, strong body. And she poised, waiting for him to move, wanting him to thrust into her.

But still he didn't. He smiled, that cheeky, boyish smile, and moved down her body. Doing once more as he'd promised, kissing her with wet, deep kisses all over her body. Only this time he did go *all* over. Until then he was kissing her there and only there—the most intimate of places. His fingers joining in too until she was rocking and pleading and about to burst. She thrashed, arms raking the sheets, not wanting it to end yet, wanting *all* of him but unable to hold herself back.

'Don't fight it,' he commanded.

And she couldn't any more. She gave in to the insistence of his mouth and fingers, lost control completely with a harsh cry. Every limb stretched long, her body arched and taut and then suddenly buckling, writhing as the tension snapped and pleasure pulsed through every cell.

Even as she was still shuddering he was moving back up her length. Kissing her stomach as it spasmed, then her screaming tight nipples were anointed by his tongue again.

He was above her now, his hand gently stroking down her jaw. She opened her eyes to find him watching her closely. She could hide nothing from him.

'You were right,' she panted. 'That was the best.'

There was no answering smile. 'No.' His eyes bored into hers, intense, serious and incredibly focused. 'That was just the beginning.'

The force of it was almost a threat. Half dizzy, she shook her head. 'I'm not sure I can…'

She felt him then, hard and thick, probing in her wetness. With a whoosh the fire inside raged back. The tiny moment of calm obliterated as the storm broke.

His hands cupped her bottom, moving her to accept him, making her mould and melt for him. She cried out at his devastating, overpowering demand.

'You can do it,' his voice encouraged gently, while his body wielded its mastery.

What she couldn't do was hold back any longer. She bent her knees, instinctively opening up more for him. She'd thought she'd been unleashed before but she'd been dreaming. Now she was beyond boundaries. There was nothing left—no thought, no shyness, no self-consciousness, no self-control as she shuddered beneath him, finally absorbing every last inch.

The rough moan that passed her lips as she arched her back was the result of raw bliss. She sighed, louder, lifting to meet him once more, unable to believe how fantastic he felt. She stroked her hand down the hard strength of his back, kissed the skin nearest to her—up and down the column of his throat, tasting the salt in the hollow of his shoulder, delighting in the way his beautiful, big body locked so completely into hers. She pressed her hips in time to meet his—again and then again, following the rhythm he set, faster and faster until finally they were moving together with a pace that was frantic, the feral sounds from her throat matched by the hoarse grunts from his. Sweat slicked them. Temperatures and sensations spiked so high that in the heat and light and speed of it all there was nothing but brilliance. Her fingers curled into claws, scouring across his skin, making him pummel so hard and so deep and so deliciously that she screamed her way to the stars and beyond.

'Open your eyes.'

She automatically obeyed. The ceiling was above her. So the world still existed. She hadn't been sure until then.

'Look at me.'

She couldn't ignore the imperative.

He had slid down the bed a bit, so his body was no longer crushing hers. Dazed, she studied the difference in their colouring. She had come from a cold winter so her skin was pale, whereas his olive complexion had been enhanced in the height of the European summer. Between her legs she could feel his strength, his heart thudding intimately against her thigh.

He was staring at her, his expression unreadable. Then a sort of smile twisted his lips. 'You're very beautiful, Emily.'

She almost smiled too but couldn't quite manage it in the tumbling emotional aftermath. 'Is it always like that for you?'

'No.'

Of course he would say that. She knew now what a gentleman he was.

His gaze dropped from hers and he pressed a kiss to her hip. 'It is never like that.'

As he spoke the words faint colour stained his cheeks and she was suddenly certain he was speaking the truth. She closed her eyes again, desperately needing to rest, to recover from the sensory overload and to deny the fleeting feeling of regret that there would be no more than this moment. He moved to lie beside her, drawing the sheet up to cover their cooling skin, bringing her head onto his chest and sliding his strong arms around her, giving her trembling body the comfort of a sure embrace.

She didn't know how long she slept. It couldn't have been that long as the sun was still high in the sky. He was awake, watching her with eyes so dark and deep they were almost all black. She didn't know *what* to say to him. How could she possibly express the intensity she'd felt?

But he shook his head slightly as if he knew. There shouldn't be words; they couldn't do it justice.

'Shower with me.' He stood from the bed and as she stared at his magnificent form the urge inside flared once more.

Her hunger must have been obvious because he smiled. 'I want to see you come again, Emily.'

She rose onto all fours, feeling the thrill of power as his eyes widened at the sight of her. 'Well, I guess that's up to you.'

The shower had never been such an exotic, erotic experience. He carried her, still connected to her, back to the bed so he could continue to manipulate her body, making her respond in a way that was fierce and passionate and almost frightening but all incredible.

For a while they lay, half-dozing, half-wrapped in towels, and through the window she watched the blue of the sky intensify. Finally she stirred, achingly stunned but also content.

'I'd better get back to the hostel.'

He didn't argue. In almost companionable silence they dressed. She drifted her way downstairs, uncaring of anyone's opinion now. None of that mattered—not in the face of this moment of bliss.

It was only when they were leaving the hotel that he spoke. 'You fly to London tomorrow?'

'Yes.' She chose not to look in his face, or at the impending reality. It was what it was, it had been shockingly wonderful, and there was nothing else to say.

Luca escorted her through the streets and fought to regain mastery over his emotions. She'd just torn every shred of self-control and reservation from him. He'd expected sweet, simple enthusiasm and he'd got a vehement passion that had rocked him to the core.

He wanted more. Oh, my God, he wanted. It was good she was going. Because despite that deep response, she was young and inexperienced and he'd be a heel to take advantage any more than he already had. The very occasional affairs he had were ultra short and he only had them with women well used to that sort of game. That wasn't Emily.

Yet the glow that had enveloped her as she lay cushioning him was like a soft, flattering light—it was how she was meant to look. Utterly beautiful and the most sensual person he'd known—and the most dangerous. Because if she could rip him open in one afternoon, what would she threaten if he saw her again? Luca had spent the best part of a decade sealing away his emotions, had zero tolerance for that kind of risk. He'd held and lost too much before and he wasn't taking the chance on it ever happening again.

Maybe he should feel guilty already but he couldn't. He'd seen the completion in her eyes—that he'd given her. It had made him feel mightier than anything. And she'd asked him for it, accepted it—understanding without asking why that this afternoon was all there could be. But, ironically, that got to him. Why didn't she want more?

She turned to him across the street from the hostel. It hung on her now, the last vestiges of satisfaction. She smiled, a serene smile that he wanted to capture and keep in his memory for ever. 'Thank you, Luca. It was the best, wasn't it?'

He nodded, unable to speak. He tilted her chin towards him with a finger, brushed her lips with his. He intended only a light kiss, a sweet goodbye to an even sweeter afternoon. But her mouth opened to him and he couldn't stop going further. And the fingers that he'd lightly rested under her chin slipped further to cup the back of her neck and pull her that little bit closer. He stroked the soft heat of her mouth with his tongue. The tiny moan in the back of her throat almost tipped him into madness.

Tearing his mouth from hers, he looked into those luminous green eyes that one last time and choked, *'Ciao, bella.'*

He turned his back to the hostel, to her, and walked. Instinctive reluctance tried to drag him back. He resisted with the determination that had seen him climb to the top of his ultra-competitive market. Yet even as he pushed his feet away he pulled out his PDA. He might not be going to see her again, but he couldn't beat the desire to ensure her arrival in London was secure—couldn't beat the need to know she was safe.

CHAPTER FIVE

THE LIGHTS of London seemed to stretch on and on. It felt as if they'd been flying over the city for hours—would they ever land? Nerves quickened Emily's pulse—part excitement, part anxiety. For the first time in her life, she had no idea what she was going to do next.

Luca dominated her thoughts. Her stiff, sore body reminded her with every tiny movement how passionate they'd been together. But she had no regrets. There was no shame or embarrassment. How could there be when it had been so natural, so right? But there was that soft romantic part of her that wished it could have lasted—could have been more. That kiss by the hostel had only refuelled her desire. She couldn't imagine having a response so absolute to anyone other than Luca.

Damn. Because Luca was in Italy and she was in England. And they would never meet again.

She forced her focus onto Kate. She was here to help her sister succeed, and succeed Kate would because she had that rare drive—there was nothing more important to her. And Emily was glad to be able to help—she'd play at her auditions, help her practise… All her adult life she'd been putting someone else first; it was easier that way. But she knew she had to sort her own problems soon, when she'd had the chance to settle Kate in. Because her life would change now; it was A.L.—*After Luca*. She smiled as the wheels of the plane touched down. For Emily, *After Luca* meant nothing would ever be the same.

As they exited the walkway from the plane Kate noticed the man holding the sign that had both their names scrawled on it. Emily approached him, heart drumming loud in her ears, wondering what on earth the message could be.

He greeted them with almost a bow and a broad smile. 'I'm under instruction to take you wherever you wish to go.'

Wherever? He was Italian. Emily's breath hitched. Could he take them back to Italy? Oh, yes, please! 'Whose instruction?' She dared not dream of the answer.

'Luca Bianchi.'

The bubble of excitement blossomed. *'Grazie,'* she replied shyly, smiling back at him. Luca had arranged this? How?

The driver's smile just went wider. He lifted their bags and led the way. Kate was giggling. It was no ordinary taxi—not a taxi at all, in fact. It was a sleek, powerful, private machine that was even bigger than the one she'd ridden in with Luca in Verona.

Emily felt a fraud pulling up outside the budget hostel in such flash wheels.

As they unloaded she didn't know whether they were supposed to tip the driver, reached for her wallet to be on the safe side.

He saw and shook his head. 'Please, Luca is a good employer but he would fire me on the spot if I took money from you.'

He lifted their packs and put them in Reception for them. Anticipation, shameless hope curled high in Emily from her toes right up to her slightly spinning head. Where was Luca? What did he want?

But there was no message, no note, no comment, *niente*—nothing. And then he was gone. The silent, smiling chauffeur, her last link to Luca, disappeared out of the door and drove away.

By the time Emily slogged up the stairs, Kate had already nabbed the top bunk and was hauling out a piece of paper. One Emily had seen too many times for comfort.

'Do you think it's too late to give this guy a call?'

'What do you think?' Emily answered, unable to hide irritation as she gestured to the window and the darkness of the night sky.

But Kate didn't even notice. 'I think it's all going to happen.' She read the note aloud for the millionth time, then asked, 'How fortunate were we to meet him?'

Emily was no longer sure. She looked at Luca's strong, bold handwriting—listing details of a very senior executive at an international recording label. She smarted inside over the way he seemed happy to pull strings for Kate and yet had made no attempt to retain contact with Emily at all. Indeed the note he'd given to Kate had been written on hotel stationery—no address or email or anything that would allow her to contact him again. He'd told her it could only be a memory—and while in her head that was fine…it wasn't fine in her heart. She couldn't stop herself from wondering…why had he sent his driver? And why then hadn't he left a message?

Being human, she found the little hurt wouldn't ease, and nor would the hope die.

'Get some sleep, Kate,' she shushed and flopped onto the bottom bunk. Trying not to talk or even think about him any more, wishing she could just put him in a box and appreciate him as that 'memory'—failing at two out of three.

Three weeks later Emily ambled along the footpath towards the hostel. She was no further ahead than when she'd first landed. By rights she should have walked into a job quickly. She'd been the one working for years— sure, it was 'only' in retail but she'd worked her way up to a managerial position and had fabulous references emphasizing her reliability. Instead it was Kate who had scored a job working in a specialist music store, found a room to rent in an apartment and she'd phoned Luca's contact—wheels were starting to turn. He'd been expecting her call, had invited her in for an audition and she'd impressed them.

So much had happened for her sister, yet for Emily herself nothing much at all. But that had been her decision. After what had happened in Italy—that taste of pleasure, the discovery of an identity away from Kate, the revelation of what she'd been missing out on—she'd realised the last thing she wanted was to recreate the life she'd had back at home. She wanted to live her own life and as part of that she didn't want to work in retail any more. All she had to do now was figure out what job she did want—not so easy. But she'd saved hard, could live frugally and so could take more time to think.

She wandered through the sights and streets, just chilling and absorbing the scene. She knew she didn't want to return to New Zealand, but she wasn't sure she'd stay in London either. So she explored the city while she could.

It was a strange feeling—the lack of responsibility. For the first time she had no one to have to cook for or care for or chase after. No hours to meet and obligations to fulfil. No real, necessary demands on her. Hadn't she been dreaming of this for so long? Finally free to observe and do nothing.

Yet alone, a little lonely, it wasn't quite as much fun as it should have been.

She heard the slam of the door nearby and turned her head. She recognised the grey car. Had to think to keep her feet walking in a straight line, then gave up, not walking at all, just watching as with deliberate steps he crossed to the footpath in front of her.

'Emily.'

That magic foreign tinge was more audible than the first time he'd spoken to her. Emily bit the inside of her cheek to stop herself moving towards him, to stop herself saying how pleased she was to see him, because she wasn't sure why he was here—was he really here?

He took another step forward and reached for her hand.

Luca. Real and vital and in a suit so sharp she had to close her eyes for a moment as his fingers curled firmly around hers.

'What are you doing here?' Were those soft words hers?

'I wanted to see how you were getting on.' His answer

came unevenly and he took in a deep breath. 'You're still living in a youth hostel.'

'Yes.'

'And yet Kate's in a flat. How did that happen?'

That was Luca, cutting straight to the chase. She could hear the condemnation in his question. He must know it all from his music business mate.

'She's young.' Emily shook her head. 'She's enjoying the freedom of adult life. Don't judge her.'

But he was. She could see the disapproval narrowing his eyes.

'What about your freedom? What were you doing when you were eighteen?'

'It was different for me. I'm pleased Kate doesn't have to deal with what I had to.' Kate had found some friends, fallen in with them so quickly, and was working hard and having fun. And why shouldn't she?

'Perhaps. But she shows not even the littlest amount of loyalty.'

'I told her to go.' Emily had never wanted to hold Kate back. Her whole aim had been to see her fly. She just hadn't realised it would happen so soon.

'She still shouldn't have. Her family should mean more to her.'

That tiny hurt part of Emily agreed with him but she couldn't voice it, couldn't admit to Kate's faults—*her* sense of loyalty wouldn't let her. The realisation that her kid sister was all grown up and no longer needed her had cut Emily to the quick. Kate had landed on her feet in this town, scored a job, settled into a flat just like that. It was

Emily who hadn't seen it coming. Emily who was still figuring out where she wanted to go and what she wanted to do…and right now she didn't need him highlighting the point. What was he doing here anyway?

'I've been in Milan.' Luca abruptly changed the subject as he saw the shadows in her eyes darken. He hadn't meant to hurt her, just wanted to know what the hell was going on. 'I returned to London late last night.' He didn't add that he'd brought forward his return by almost a week because he couldn't wait any longer to see her again. And now that he had, he could hardly wait to hold her again. Every fibre in him wanted to pull her close. He wanted to see fire in her eyes—not the tinge of pain he could see there now.

But she'd frozen up. Maybe he shouldn't have mentioned Kate yet but he'd been stunned to hear about her moving in with some other wannabe musos and leaving Emily high and dry. He'd sent his driver to the airport so she'd get to her hostel safely, right? But really it had been so he'd find out where she was staying. All along, deep inside, he'd known he had to see her again.

'Returned to London? Right,' she said with bite. 'I thought you lived in Italy.'

He hadn't even told her that. A prickle of remorse roughened his answer. 'I mostly live in London but spend a lot of time in Milan—I go to Verona from there.'

She nodded, but he wasn't sure she'd heard him all that well. 'Why didn't you tell me that before?'

'There wasn't really time.' It was a pathetic excuse and he knew she knew it as well as he.

'Why didn't you try to contact me? You didn't even ask for an email address or a phone number or anything.' Mottled pink colour was slowly sweeping across her skin.

'I wanted it to be over.' His blood was pumping faster too and his senses were more acute—he couldn't tear his gaze from her.

'So why are you here now?' She was trembling; he could feel the tremors through her fingers.

'Because I missed you.' Every muscle in him tensed at the admission—at the desire. He knew her body moulded perfectly to his and he had to fight to stop himself pulling her close.

'And?' Was it anger or passion stirring her eyes to that emerald-green?

He couldn't resist her, couldn't stop the words tearing from him, low and harsh. 'Because I wanted to see you again.'

'You're seeing me now.'

'You know what I mean.'

'What, you want to have your wicked way with me again?' She tossed her head to glare at him, all spirit and spark.

'*Wicked?*' He challenged her right back.

She closed her eyes at that. 'Wild.'

It had been one wild, wonderful afternoon. He denied any wickedness—they had both wanted it. They both still did—he just had to get her to admit that too. Another tumble with her was all he wanted. As much as he hated to admit it, once hadn't been enough. 'Say yes, Emily, and we could do that again.'

* * *

Emily battled the satisfaction thrilling through her. He still wanted her. He'd come after her for that very purpose.

Unrelenting need.

Hadn't she been aching with it for days now? But she tried to let rational thought have a moment of supremacy over that most basic instinct governing her. This was different. This might lead to a mess. As it was she'd been feeling below par. It had to be different this time—there had to be more.

She breathed deep, spoke carefully. 'That afternoon was so complete. So perfect. Should we run the risk of ruining the memory of it?'

'Yes.' Decisive. Emphatic. No hesitation in his reply.

'Why?'

He stepped even closer. 'Because it wasn't complete. It wasn't perfect.' His head lowered towards hers. 'We were left wanting.'

Her lips tingled, his were so very near and the rush of memories was mixing with the present. It felt so natural and right for her to tilt that little bit further forward.

Her mouth touched his, clung to the warmth. Would have parted further and let him in if he'd made the move. But he lifted away, just a fraction, and she barely controlled the moan of disappointment, failed to suppress the sigh. *Frustration.*

His smile was slight, and his eyes were dark with determination. 'See?'

There were commuters rushing all around them. Staring straight ahead, pacing along the footpath, keen to get home, to after-work assignations, to the gym, to whatever it was that they were looking forward to after a long day at the office. But in their tiny patch of the universe, less than a metre square, there was stillness, save their slow breathing.

'Let's get dinner.' His mouth hardly moved as he spoke.

'I'm not really dressed for dinner.' She didn't want to be dressed at all. His gaze frisked her. She knew he'd caught her thought and she also knew his reply. He'd be happy to eat there and then and she was the dish of the day.

'Dinner. Tonight. Now.' He seemed to have lost the ability to form whole sentences.

'OK.' Just as she had lost the ability to think at all.

As she stared out of the window Emily's whole body quivered, tightening with the thrill of remembered ecstasy. She could only hear the rush of her pulse, not the reason of her mind. A tiny part of her was tense with warning, but the rest tense with longing. He was staring ahead at the road, his face shadowed by a frown, concentrating harder than the slow-moving traffic warranted.

'Have you been busy with work?' Oh, it was inane, but she had to break the taut silence somehow.

'Very,' came the brief reply. Then he too seemed to make the effort. 'It's always pretty busy. But things have been really hectic the last couple of weeks.' He glanced at her. 'What about you? Have you found a job?'

'I haven't really been looking. I'm still deciding what I want to do so I've just been cruising.'

'Are you enjoying not working?'

'Well, I don't miss being on my feet all day.' She laughed. 'It's weird not having to be anywhere at a prescribed hour.'

Or having anyone to talk to. She'd easily spent more than one day not talking to anyone in this city of millions.

'How have you been filling your days?'

'Just walking. Sightseeing. There are lots of sights in London.'

'So you are still on your feet all day,' he teased.

'It's a little different.' She grinned.

She watched him drive, his sure, calm control of the machine. It wasn't long before they were back in the heart of the city. He pulled into a parking space, escorted her with his innate politeness to the door. Unlocking it, he swung the heavy wood wide, before pressing a security keypad on the inside wall. She stepped forward into the surprisingly light foyer and looked at the calm colours, the polished wooden floor. Spacious, with high ceilings, wide doorways, and a long staircase, his house was beautiful. He didn't stop to give her the tour, led her straight to the airy kitchen at the back of the ground floor, where he fiddled with buttons on the oven. Then he reached into a cupboard, drawing out a bottle of red with one hand and tossing her a box of grissini with the other. And she watched—every sure movement of his strong body. His large, confident hands worked the cork out of the bottle, the glass fitted snugly into his palm as he poured generously. He had beautiful hands. He had beautiful everything.

She kept watching as he pulled out a tray from the oven—smothered in vegetables, roasted to perfection and a joint of meat resting in the middle. Her mouth was watering but it wasn't because of the food.

'Just a little something you prepared earlier?' she asked, amazed.

A half-smile twinkled. 'I have a housekeeper—Micaela. She works every weekday. On weekends when necessary.'

Of course he had hired help. That was OK. It had still been his idea—like the picnic in Verona. Memories haunted her muscles. Emily fiddled with the box of grissini—anything to keep her hands from fiddling with him. The ache inside was becoming a pain now. He was here, he was so close and she *wanted*.

'You hungry?' he asked, watching the tray as he lifted it to the bench.

'Mmm-hmm.' She couldn't trust herself to speak. Her voice already felt rusty, desire corroding it.

He turned, lanced her with his all-seeing eyes and spoke dryly. 'Don't hold back, Emily.'

She broke free of his piercing gaze, ripped at the box and grabbed a breadstick as others spilled across the bench.

He took the two steps to get right into her space. She couldn't not look at him then. He knew. She knew he understood the depth of her need. And as if to prove it his fingers lightly danced down her throat, sliding down her chest until his palm moved to cup her swollen breast, thumb tormenting her taut nipple as it had those few weeks ago.

The breadstick snapped between her fingers.

His face lit up with that smile. His other hand slid up her leg then, under her skirt all the way up to her knickers. They were no barrier and she gasped in pleasure as his fingers slipped under the elastic, testing and instantly moving to tease as he felt the full extent of her appetite.

'Luca...'

'If you're hungry, Emily,' he instructed solemnly, 'you should *never* hold back.'

So she didn't—couldn't. Her insides were like lava. Her deeply hidden core that she'd always thought firm and cool, rational and sensible, was now molten, blistering hot and bending her towards him. Driving her. Rocking her pelvis into his hand, she met his mouth with hers open and needy, her hands moving, fighting to touch him—going straight for the kill.

He groaned as his fingers stroked deep. 'I've been wanting this again since the moment I left you in Verona.'

'So what took you so long?'

'I'm stubborn.'

'Why do you want to fight it?' Panting, she unzipped his trousers with a rough jerk. Got her hands on him the way he had his on her—intimate and demanding.

Everything was unleashed. The kiss was hard and passionate and their hands provoked even more until they were both shaking. Teeth scraped and tongues thrust and yet for her they were nowhere near close enough or fast enough or *anything* enough. She growled as he tore his lips from hers.

'This isn't how...' He looked into her eyes and the fire arced between them—incandescent and unstoppable.

With a smile she hooked an arm around his neck and pulled him to meet her open, hungry mouth. Moments, minutes, hours lost in another kiss so passionate it almost hurt.

He whipped his hands from her body and she rolled onto

her toes, only just keeping her balance. His hands came back—hard on her arms. 'No. We should talk first. And before we do that we should eat.'

'I'm not in imminent danger of fading away—let's talk now.' Frustration made her snappy.

He stared hard at her. 'This can only be a fling, Emily. That's all I can offer.'

'Why?' Why put limits on this before it had really begun—why not just see where it went?

Silence.

She watched the darkness grow in his eyes. 'Did someone hurt you, Luca?'

His hands tightened on her arms. 'Badly.'

'I won't hurt you.' She liked him. She'd like to get to know him more.

'I know.' A blunt response. 'Because I won't let you.' His grip loosened, fingers skimmed down to her wrists. 'But I don't want to hurt you either.'

'Who says you will?' She placed the palms of her hands on his chest. His arrogant assumption that he might annoyed her. Defensive pride reared its head. 'Maybe all I want from you is *just* this—no-holds-barred sex and nothing else.'

He glared back, the frown drowning in a glower of epic proportions. 'OK,' he said. 'Seeing we're being honest, let me put it plain. I don't do relationships. I don't do commitment. I've been married once before and I will *never* do it again.'

She tightened her muscles, absorbing the shock, but his brutal honesty continued.

'No commitment, Emily. No strings. Do you still want this, knowing that?'

She stared hard into the darkness of his eyes, let hers roam over his features, his olive skin, the angled jaw that right now was shadowed with stubble, the full mouth.

Just a few nights of mind-bending passion?

It was already too late.

'Didn't I just say that? No-holds-barred sex and nothing else? Let's say I think of you as my holiday fling.'

'You're sure?'

'Yes.'

'Then that's it.' He vanquished all possibility of any further thought with a few words and a lot of action. His hands intimately invaded her body, his mouth pressed bruisingly hard on hers blocking everything but sensation.

Passion, born of pent-up need and sudden anger, had her go straight for the zenith too—hands back hard on the thing she wanted right inside her. Pulling him closer, firmer, faster.

A breathless second apart as he pulled a condom from his pocket, tearing the foil open and forcing the rubber on. And almost fully clothed, their dinner waiting, they surged together. Frantic, fast—both desperately fighting for that fix of pleasure.

It was mere seconds in coming—their bodies clenched together like vices, racked with violent shudders.

After the echo of her screams passed, it was their breathing—short, sharp, harsh—that filled her ears.

She opened her eyes, looked straight into his—where a

flicker of rue nestled. 'Wow,' he muttered. 'I'm thinking that was the appetiser.'

She took a deep breath, stepped back, rested her weight on her hands on the bench behind her and tried to act completely cool—as if this sort of meltdown were nothing out of the ordinary. 'I'm looking forward to the main course.'

His brows lifted. 'While I'm looking forward to dessert.'

She flushed—she hadn't meant… He caught her eye and winked. Her colour still burning, she turned away and adjusted her clothing. When she'd summoned the courage and calm to turn back, he'd done the same.

He concentrated on serving—quick and efficient. She just focused on breathing and standing upright. He looked across at her. 'Are you OK?'

She nodded. 'I think so.'

He shook his head. 'Let's eat, OK?'

The dinner was divine, the meat melt-in-the-mouth tender, the vegetables tangy with some sort of marinade, but her mind was spinning too fast for her to truly enjoy it.

He held his fork with his left hand, using his right to cover hers—curling his fingers around hers. It wasn't a possessive grip, nor demanding in a sexual way. It was simple contact. Almost comfort. And she appreciated it, needing the connection. While there was to be nothing long-lasting between them, she needed to know there was some sort of caring.

'Have you got a mobile?'

'I picked up a prepay last week.' To field calls from employment agencies she'd yet to sign up with. To stay in contact with her sister who was too busy to bother.

'I'll give you my number.' He stood, pushed the plates away and pulled her into his arms. 'I'm not settling for a morsel this time. I'm having the whole banquet.'

Drugging kisses led to all-consuming passion, he carried her up the stairs to a room that was light and fresh and utterly impersonal.

She glanced, vision blurry. 'This isn't your room?'

'My room's a mess. I couldn't let you see it with all my stuff all over the floor.' And then he kissed her more, all over, confusing her thoughts, until she no longer cared about anything but having him inside her.

But after, as she lay loose-limbed and replete, she started to wonder what was going to happen next. She decided to test the waters. 'I should get back to the hostel.'

He lay beside her, said nothing.

'All my things are there,' she couldn't stop adding.

'I'll take you.'

She shouldn't feel the thump of disappointment when she'd been prepared. But it walloped her in the stomach all the same. He didn't want her to stay—not even the rest of the night. It really was just the fulfilment of an urge—scratching the itch and all that.

He left to change and she quickly pulled on her clothes, refusing to let emptiness eat away her satisfaction. Finding her way back down to the living area, she hardened her heart. This was her treat, remember? This was her chance to have and take what *she* wanted—and she had wanted. And she *still* wanted.

He was already waiting for her. In jeans and tee—she'd never seen him in jeans and, oh, yes, he was still her treat.

They drove back to the hostel in silence. Pulling up outside, he unclicked his seat belt.

'Don't come in,' she said hurriedly, not wanting awkwardness to swallow the last remnants of pleasure.

He didn't kiss her this time, just looked at her with shadowed, burning eyes that seemed to touch her skin just as if they were his lips anyway. 'I'll be in touch.'

CHAPTER SIX

THE more Luca thought about it, the more he didn't like it. And he spent all day thinking about it. Emily couldn't stay there, but the solution was no more tolerable—either way he was confronted with a situation he wasn't comfortable with. But inevitably, as it had once already, desire won. He strode into the hostel common room wearing jeans and a shirt and a scowl. 'Get your bag.'

'Pardon?' She was sitting cross-legged on a sofa, eating toast and reading the paper—at nine-thirty at night.

'You shouldn't be staying here. It's not safe.'

'Not safe?'

'No,' he asserted, feeling all the more grumpy. 'Not safe. Full of transients and people you don't know. I wouldn't let my sister stay in a place like this on her own.'

'Do you have a sister?'

'No, but if I did, I wouldn't let her stay here.'

'You wouldn't *let* her?'

He ignored the emphasis. 'Come on, get your bag. You're coming home with me.'

'Do you have a brother?'

'No. But again, if I did, I wouldn't want him staying here. Not if I could convince him otherwise. It's not right for a lone woman to stay here.' He paced in a circle. 'When you were with your sister it was different—just. But not now.'

She stepped in front of him, blocking his path. 'And you don't think moving in with some stranger is more risky?'

A flash of surprise checked him. 'I'm not a stranger. And you know you have nothing to fear from me.'

He watched her think about it. Watched her sleepy, luminescent eyes widen.

'Save your money and stay with me.' He knew he almost had it won. He added some frills. 'I'm your holiday fling, right? Why not let me provide the whole package—room, food and entertainment? Take your time to decide on a job and a flat. I don't mind.'

'Why, how generous you are, Luca,' she drawled. 'And what do you get out of it?'

'What we're both counting on.' His house was his sanctuary. Quiet, relaxing—his and his alone. But for a few days he'd have to adjust. His body's need was too strong—breaking through the boundaries he'd established years ago. And he couldn't rest knowing she was alone in this hostel. Privacy and isolation could be restored—after.

'You know I can't say no.'

'I was counting on that too.'

Did she really have nothing to fear? A little doubt niggled in the back of Emily's brain. No strings, no commitment—wouldn't living together make it harder to keep that distance? But she couldn't resist his offer—and it *was* generous. Even though she was a with-it woman living in the twenty-first century and totally capable of safely staying in the hostel all by herself, she couldn't help her instinctive, pleased response to his display of macho protectiveness. And while it might not be that risky, it was certainly reckless. Reckless was something Emily hadn't ever been until that day in Verona. That hedonism, the holiday mood enveloped her now—bringing back the warmth of the Italian sun, the taste of bliss in his arms... Why couldn't she extend that holiday, just for a little while longer? Didn't, as he'd once said, she deserve it?

'Your room, ma'am.'

He put her pack inside the door of the bedroom they'd lain in last night. The guest bedroom. So boundaries would be maintained—she wouldn't actually be sleeping in *his* bed. She crossed the room and looked out of the window—last night she hadn't been lucid enough to notice the view over the private gated gardens.

'I'll show you where the key is. You can go and read the morning paper in the sun. It's very nice.' He took her hand. 'Let me show you the rest of the facilities. You've seen the kitchen and you have your own bathroom off your bedroom, so let's move on to entertainment.'

'I thought you were my entertainment.'

'I'll entertain you again and again. But this is for while I'm at work.'

And, if last night was anything to go by, it would be her recovery time. She followed him into the big, light room. A large sofa stretched in front of her and opposite was a wall of bookcases.

'Take your pick, but if you don't fancy reading…' He pushed a couple of buttons on a remote and with a click and a whir half the bookcases seemed to disappear and a giant flat-screen TV was revealed.

'Oh, that's clever.'

'Very Batman, don't you think?' he joked. 'The DVDs are in this cabinet. I have a reasonable collection, but if you want to watch something else just let me know and I can get it delivered.'

A reasonable collection? There were masses of DVDs— enough to rival the entire stock of the DVD store where she'd worked. Although they were a little on the action/thriller side. Not too many romcom chick flicks— maybe his ex took them when they split up? She felt burningly curious about that part of his life—what had gone wrong? She'd ask some time, but was cautious about prying too much too soon. There had been real pain in his eyes when he'd admitted to being hurt and she didn't want to spoil the lightness of the mood now. Not when she sensed this was a little out of the ordinary for him. It was way out of the ordinary for her too.

'I take them out of the cases. It makes it easier to store more.'

'And are they filed alphabetically, by genre, or director or something?'

'No.' He grinned. 'In order of purchase. By all means sort them if you want, though. Watch any, watch all.'

'You expect me to figure out all these remote controls? The stereo, the TV, the DVD player, the *curtains*…'

He laughed and gestured towards the bi-folding doors

along the back wall. 'Through there is a formal lounge I don't tend to use unless I have some sort of gathering. Now follow. I've saved the best 'til last.'

His room? She was *very* curious about that. But while he led her to the stairs it wasn't up but down that he went. At the very bottom they were confronted with a closed door. He pushed buttons on the keypad on the wall beside them. 'I'll give you the number.'

'I'm going to need a two-hundred-page manual to re-member how to work this place.'

'It won't take you that long.'

'Why the security?'

'My housekeeper has a young son. I don't want him in here without supervision.'

'Supervision?' What on earth was in there? 'And you said I had nothing to fear? Let me guess, it's a soundproof room and filled with electric guitars and drum kit 'cos you're really a metal head.'

He shook his head.

'Wine cellar?'

He grinned. 'I have a couple of cabinets upstairs but the bulk of my collection is stored offsite.'

He was serious about that?

'Believe it or not this is much more fun.' He opened the door.

She blinked as he switched on the lights. Oh, wow. She would never have expected this.

The expanse of blue was lit underneath—the light was subtle and it was warm and cast pretty patterns on the gleaming white walls.

'Oh.' The water was about two lanes wide and went the length of the room.

'There's a small gym down there and a bathroom through there.' He walked down the last step onto the small paved area at the head of the pool. 'Nice, huh?' He whipped off his tee shirt, and kicked away his shoes. His hands went to his belt.

'Very nice.' Her smile broadened as he pulled his jeans down and stepped out of them. His boxers followed. 'Really, very nice.'

He winked back, then turned, dived straight in, his arms moving in a perfect arc. He surfaced several feet out in the pool, droplets of water flew as he shook his head. 'Aren't you coming in?'

She stood at the edge and thought of the lamest excuse she could. 'I don't have my swimsuit with me.'

'Emily, this is hardly the public pools. You don't need a swimsuit.'

Time for honesty, then. 'Actually, I'm not the most confident swimmer.'

'You come from an island nation. I thought you were all born swimming.'

'I can swim. I'm just not that confident. I don't like it when my feet can't touch the bottom. It looks really deep there.'

'It is really deep. But I can make it shallower for you.'

'How?'

'It has an adjustable floor. I can't do it right now, but will do later if you want.'

Adjustable floor? 'Why do you have it so deep?'

'I like diving.'

'As in somersaults and flips and stuff?'

'No, as in scuba- and free diving. I practise down here. Have you ever gone scuba diving? Underwater gardens are as beautiful as the trees and flowers sort.'

'I don't think that's for me.' She shook her head. 'I'd be afraid of being swallowed whole and never finding my way to the surface.'

'It's easy. Come on, come in. It's really shallow this end. Think of it as a giant bath.'

It was too beautiful to resist. Just like him.

'I'm not going in that deep end.' She tried not to feel self-conscious as she stripped, felt better as he swam closer, looking more wicked the more naked she became.

She stepped down the ladder. It *was* a giant bath—but tepid, neither too cold nor too warm.

'You're not a risk-taker?' He reached out for her.

'I haven't been in a position to be able to take risks.' She let him pull her through the water.

'But you're in a position to now.'

Yes. And she already was taking a huge risk.

The floor of the pool suddenly dropped away.

'Hold onto me.' He put her arms around his neck. Their bodies bumped, warm and wet, and she wound her legs round his waist. His legs worked, keeping them both afloat, moving them through the water.

'Does nothing scare you?' she asked. He seemed so strong, so sure of himself.

'The things that scare me are the things that happen outside of my control but that impact on my life.'

'What—like hurricanes?' She felt his puff of laughter.

'Hurricanes of the human kind.'

'Like losing your mum?'

'Yeah, I guess.' No laughter this time.

'What was boarding school like?' She still couldn't get over that one—how isolated he must have been.

'Actually it wasn't that bad. It wasn't an archetypal horror. I had good teachers, stability—year in, year out same place, same people. My father provided the money for a first-class education and all the extras I could want. Swimming, skiing, scuba. I studied hard but I had a good time too. More of a good time than you probably did. Was there no one else for you and Kate?'

'Mum had a brother but he lived hours away and wasn't able to help. We were OK. I had Kate.' She looked down into the blue; it really was very deep beneath them. 'You like going down there?'

'I like the quiet. The weightlessness. Free of encumbrances.'

'You've got an encumbrance now.'

'You weigh nothing in the water, Emily.' He grinned. 'I'll help you go below and then find the surface again. You'll be swimming like a mermaid in no time.'

They were heading back towards the end of the pool and she swam away from him to the edge.

'I might be a mermaid who plays in the shallows.' She climbed up the ladder, chanced a look at him over her shoulder and burst out laughing.

He stood, the water lapping at his hips, his erection thrusting from the water like some sort of missile, and his face bore the expression of a satyr.

'I'm thinking you're more of a siren than a mermaid.'
He didn't bother with the ladder, simply vaulted over the
side and lunged for her. 'You're going to like the shower
down here.'

Emily slept for longer than she'd ever slept in her life.
When conscious at last, she lay quietly listening for sounds
of movement, but he must have gone to work hours ago.
She showered in the spacious en suite, standing for a long
time under the hot, heavy jet of water, washing away the
faint aches from Luca's all-physical passion. Slowly she
dressed, unsure of what she wanted to do today. She hadn't
had a holiday since she was a kid. And now she had the time
to consider her options—to work out what her options even
were. Stomach rumbling, she headed straight to the kitchen.

As she entered the room she could suddenly hear a noise
nearby. The door to the walk-in pantry was shut, but the
door beside it was open. Emily went through and looked
at the stranger in the middle of the small room she'd hadn't
even known was there. She was a petite woman who looked
as if she'd swallowed a beach ball—pregnant as anything.

'You must be Emily.' She spoke, a pretty Italian accent
colouring her words. 'I'm Micaela.'

The tiny brunette was drowning in sheets. Some
complex ironing contraption in front of her and a wall of
high thread count all round.

Emily nodded. Amazed at the scene, she took in the
sound of the washing machine and the dryer beside it.

'I can make my bed,' Emily said hurriedly as she looked
at the sheet mountain. 'Please.'

Micaela smiled. 'You are staying in—'

'The room with that incredible view over the gardens.' She wondered if the view from the floor above would be even more spectacular... Luca's own personal space.. what was it like?

Emily looked at the housekeeper again, worried. She was tiny and pregnant and shouldn't be scrubbing the floors or wrestling with the ironing or anything much, surely.

'Can I help you with those?' She automatically stepped in, taking one end of the sheet and helping to fold the smooth linen.

'Don't worry,' Micaela assured her as they stacked the folded sheet on top of the others. 'My husband usually helps and he does any heavy work. You've met him already. Ricardo. He drove you from the airport.'

Oh. That was her husband? So they both worked for Luca. And Micaela knew about the airport ride. Emily wondered what she made of it—wondered if it was normal for Luca to pick up strange women when overseas.

'Luca thinks I should stop working altogether, but I like to keep busy. So—' Micaela stepped out from behind the mass of white and led the way back to the kitchen '—what can I get you for lunch?'

'Oh. Nothing.' Emily was embarrassed on several levels—she wasn't used to someone preparing food for her, and was it really lunchtime already? 'I'll make myself a sandwich later. And I promise I'll clean up after.'

Micaela's smile was almost friendly. 'Well, if you need anything, please just let me know.'

'Thank you,' Emily murmured awkwardly. She drifted

through a door and found herself in the formal lounge that Luca had gestured to last night. A gleaming black baby grand piano stood showcased in the corner. She was instantly drawn to it. Happiness flooded her—she hadn't played properly in weeks. She ran a finger along the edge—not a speck of dust. She doubted that Luca played— it didn't seem to fit his image somehow. But owning one that was so magnificent didn't surprise her. Luca had nothing but the best.

Gingerly she sat at the piano seat, a little in awe, and experimented with a key here and there, then a chord. It was perfectly tuned. But she sensed this instrument hadn't been played properly in a long time. She stretched her fingers out, feeling the pressure of the piano resisting her. She pushed harder on the keys and then softer to get the right tone. Her foot tentatively touched the pedals.

The sound she wanted started to come. And then she forgot her surroundings—simply sat and played as she hadn't in years. Not the accompaniment to one of Kate's songs—beautiful as they were—but a solo piece, just for her own pleasure.

A step sounded right behind her. Emily spun on the seat. Nearly fell off it as she saw the small boy only a nose away watching her. So much for thinking she had any sort of sixth sense. How long had he been standing there?

'Hi,' she said. He must be the housekeeper's son and rather gorgeous he was too.

He said nothing in reply. His eyes darted to the piano behind her.

'Want to hear some more?'

He didn't answer, but he looked like a yes. Emily smiled. He was cute.

'Come on, then.' She turned back to the keyboard, not wanting to make him more self-conscious and run away. She launched straight into another piece—one that he might recognise. A few minutes later she felt his restlessness at her side. She glanced at him—was he over it already? Had enough? Itching to get away? But no, he was watching her fingers on the keys and she realised the restlessness was his own little fingers moving.

'You want to have a go?'

There was a smile then.

At first she had palpitations over some kid's sticky fingers bashing the keys. But it was built to be played—to be used, to be loved. And she could tell by the roundness of his eyes that this was something he'd wanted for a while.

Her smile grew as wide as his as she guided his fingers and they tapped out 'Twinkle Twinkle'. He giggled. She understood exactly how he felt.

'Marco.'

He jumped. So did Emily.

'It's OK.' Emily turned quickly to speak to Micaela. She didn't want him to get in trouble. But then she saw the indulgence in his mother's eyes and knew there was no way this boy could ever do anything bad as far as she was concerned. She said something softly to him in Italian that had him running out of the room.

'Thank you,' Micaela said.

'It's nice to have someone who likes to listen,' Emily said simply. 'How old is he?'

'Almost five. He'll be starting school in a couple of weeks.'

Emily nodded. 'He's lovely.' She felt braver now, able to talk. 'When are you due?'

'December.' Micaela's smile was different this time, full and unreserved. 'Our own little Christmas miracle.'

By the time Luca got home—late—Emily's need, like a fever, had her hot and jumpy. Passion was the only cure for the madness bubbling her blood—unfortunately, it was also the cause. She met him at the door and the look in his eye mirrored hers—ravenous. Melting against him, she savagely ran her fingers through his hair. They dropped to the floor, keeping the contact of the kiss as much as they could. Unashamedly she stretched out, spreading her legs, arching up as he pressed down on her, his hands forcing fabric aside. He thrust deep as she was still undoing the top button on his shirt, only just getting him naked enough for her to curl her nails into his skin as the spasms hit and she came.

'Not enough,' he growled, rocking harder into her. 'I want it to last…' But instead he groaned as she clamped tight around him, flexing her feminine muscles to trap and release him hard and fast and revelling as he finally collapsed.

Lying beneath him, she forced herself to ignore the burgeoning feelings that now followed so fast after the physical relief. She had to remember what they'd agreed. She had to keep it carefree.

'So, honey—' she put on a cooing tone '—did you have a good day?'

CHAPTER SEVEN

'PLAY the elephant one again.'

'OK,' Emily laughed. 'But you have to do the singing.'

She and Marco were having a fine time at the piano. Giggling over Emily's deliberately wrong notes and the game of starting over again.

'What's going on?' Luca didn't sound anywhere near as amused as they were.

Marco leapt off the seat but Emily refused to jump to attention. She slowly turned. What was he doing home in the middle of the day?

'We're playing the piano.' Coolly she answered with the obvious.

'Marco.' Micaela was at the doorway in a blink and her son scarpered from the room. Emily saw the anxious glance the housekeeper sent Luca. She didn't blame her. There was something in his silent appraisal that had her feeling uncomfortable too. But she wasn't going to let it show. Luca might be the boss of Micaela, but he wasn't the boss of her. She was his guest—wasn't she? Not an employee to be told off for insubordination or overstepping the mark.

Micaela said something in Italian. He gave only a brief reply, a flash of teeth and then the woman stepped back. She sent a small smile in Emily's direction, but Emily barely saw it, too busy trying to read the unreadable mask that was Luca's face and growing all the more irritated with her failure.

Luca heard the door click and knew Micaela had headed to the kitchen. He stepped further into the lounge, unable to take his eyes off Emily, unable to stop the churning feeling inside.

For the forty-six thousandth time he asked himself what he was doing. Jerked his shoulders because he had no idea and it irritated him. He couldn't have left her at that hostel, he'd been right to bring her here—a week or so, she'd get sorted and they'd burn themselves out. But he hadn't had enough of her. If anything his desire was growing. Only two days into it and here he was at home in the middle of the day because he wanted to *see* her, wanted to talk to her, wanted to spend time with her.

With wary movements she turned a little to the side and gestured. 'It's a beautiful piano. I hope you don't mind.'

'No.' She looked disconcerted at his bald reply and he forced himself to elaborate. 'I used to sit by my mother when she played.' It was one of the few happy memories he had of her before the sickness had struck.

'Was this hers?'

'No. My father got rid of it not long after her death. This is the one she should have had.'

'Is that why you have it?'

'I needed something to fill the space.' He shrugged. 'I didn't know you played.'

'I've accompanied Kate for years.'

Of course she had—literally, emotionally. Only now Kate no longer needed her. 'Will you play for me?' He wanted to sit where Marco had.

'Maybe later.' She closed the lid.

He was going to take her out to lunch. This was her first trip to London and so far she hadn't exactly had the best tour of it. It wasn't so much fun seeing the sights on your own. He didn't bother when he travelled for work, just focused on the job. But he felt a whim to see Emily enjoy London; he wanted to see how beautiful she was as she explored it. Only now that idea went right out the window as he stared at her, sitting at his piano.

'You were wearing that tee shirt at the Arena.' Her eyes were that bright green. His mouth went dry, senses homed in on one thing only—her. The need was stronger than ever. He stepped closer, watching her reaction—he could see her breathing accelerate, see her breasts tighten and her mouth part.

Sì.

He took her face in both hands, caressed her high, smooth cheekbones with his thumbs before bending close. Sliding his fingers into her hair, he looked into her flushed features, at her gleaming, dilated eyes, and raw satisfaction kicked as she leant back towards him—seeking.

This was what he wanted. He scooped her up and carried her straight up to her room, hooking her door shut behind him with his foot.

As he set her down she mumbled beneath his mouth, 'Micaela...Marco.'

'They won't hear us.' And he made sure of it by simply placing his lips back over hers and keeping them there. Kissing and connecting deep. And all the while he refused to think, refused to analyse why it was that when he was sealed together with her like this, his very soul seemed to soar. He just wanted to fly.

Emily drew the sheet over her and watched as he stepped into the en suite bathroom and showered briefly before dressing. He looked a different man from the dark angel who had appeared before. Now his expression was lighter; he was smiling as he pulled his trousers back on.

'Is that what you came home for?'

'Actually, no.' He grinned. 'But there's always tomorrow. And—' a quick kiss on her lips '—I'll be back tonight.' He was out of the door before she had the chance to ask more.

Moments later she heard him speaking in Italian, heard the higher-pitched tones as Micaela answered. Emily winced. He'd still been doing up his belt as he'd left her room. It couldn't have been more obvious that they'd had a tryst. That he was a satisfied man. And for the first time in their affair, a trickle of embarrassment crept in.

What had that been all about if not purely for a lunchtime quickie? Never mind that she'd revelled in it—loving the sense of closeness that had come with all the kissing. But it wasn't real, was it, that closeness? That had just been to stop them shouting and making even more of an awkward situation with Micaela and her son in the rooms below. All it was to Luca was the sex. There was no hint of involvement with his life—no dates, no suggestion of going out to dinner, no plans to see or do anything...

Wasn't she good enough for even a little romance? Couldn't he at least play at it as he had that day in Verona— with his posh picnic and fine wine and saucy sweet talk? Or did he think he didn't need to bother any more? That he knew she'd put out for him the minute he so much as looked at her?

And it was true. Damn it. She would. Because nothing on earth had ever felt as good as having Luca in her bed, in her arms and in her body.

She waited in her room until she was sure Micaela and Marco would have left for the day. Then she walked—for hours along the river, trying to figure out how to fix the crack that was appearing in the holiday fling. She didn't want it to end but she might have to reset the rules.

Luca got home as soon as he could without officially declaring it a holiday. Who was he kidding? His brain had gone AWOL days ago. And after leaving her earlier, he had taken a detour. Another whim, another moment of madness. He'd wanted to find something for her. In his mind's eye he'd seen her playing the piano, in that old worn shirt and thin skirt, her bare arms and naked fingers making such music. He'd never felt jealous of a four-year-old boy before but he'd have given anything to sit where Marco had been sitting and be the beneficiary of that beautiful smile and all that attention.

He had the even stronger desire to take a few days off and take her on a jaunt—truly make it a holiday. But as that idea teased he clenched his teeth hard together; mentally he inked the line and underlined it again. Too damn dangerous. Already he was in a position he'd vowed never to let happen—he had a lover who'd lasted more than a few dates and, worse, she was staying in his own home. And while he was trying to maintain much of his usual distance, every day it was eroding and the desire to keep distant was eroding fast with it.

He had to fight harder. He had to finish this sooner rather than later because the one thing he refused to risk again was getting close to anyone. Because he always lost out, didn't he? Those he loved never stuck around. Losing Nikki had been the worst thing that had ever happened to him. In no way was he up for anything like a repeat. He wanted some fun now, he'd earned it with all the years of nothing but work, but fun was all it could be.

But when he walked in and found Emily was out, disappointment hit him heavy in the chest. He sat at the kitchen counter and opened another box of the grissini he'd got Micaela to find especially for her. Gnawing on the breadstick, he appreciated it for the displacement activity it was.

He glanced at his watch and then out at the sky. Not long now and the darkness would fall completely. Maybe she'd gone to see Kate. Maybe she'd left him? At that thought he went to her room and felt relief gush as he saw her pack still there, small items still scattered on the table.

And then irritation mopped all the good feeling up. Well, where was she, then? And what was he doing even worrying about it? *This* was what he didn't want. He didn't want to be so concerned about someone else; he was comfort-eating breadsticks while he waited for her. He didn't want to wait for anybody. He didn't want to be sitting around letting someone else mess with his emotions.

He poured wine, drank it, decided to give her 'til nine and then he'd start walking the neighbourhood.

Ten minutes later the key scraped against the door and he raced to jerk it open.

'Where have you been?' he positively barked, and then had to take a breath and remind himself to chill out.

'Walking.' She looked surprised. 'I didn't think you'd be home this early.'

'Oh.' Ordinarily he wasn't. But ordinarily his ultimate temptation wasn't waiting for him on his sofa.

Except she hadn't been. She'd been out somewhere and now she looked knackered. 'Come and eat. You look done in.'

She sat at the counter and helped herself to the grissini as he poured a large glass of red. He let her sip and munch while he pulled a salad from the fridge, tossed some onto a plate for her, and broke some bread to put alongside it. 'Where did you go?'

She shrugged. 'For a walk down by the river.' She crunched for another moment. 'It's a lovely night. Lots of people spilling out of pubs.'

'You didn't go in?'

'Not on my own, no.'

He hadn't been down that way in ages. She was right, he wasn't usually home by now—still working, watching the US markets, and then when they closed those in Asia were almost due to open again… He glanced out of the window. It was a warm night—a drink by the river would be nice.

Then he remembered his mild panic when she hadn't been home—not nice—and so he held back the whim. He'd succumbed to two of those already today. He set down a platter of cheese and meat for her to pick at as well as the salad.

'Have you spoken to Kate at all?' She should go out with her sister. Then he wouldn't have either this niggle of guilt or this leap of temptation.

'No.' She kept her eyes on the plates. 'She's busy.'

Busy being self-absorbed.

But he didn't go there, he let her eat, told her some lame scuba story. When she'd finished he whisked away her plate. 'Come on, let's go somewhere comfortable.'

She did look tired. He wanted to make her smile—he hoped he had just the thing. He led her to the lounge and nudged her onto the sofa and went to the stereo to choose some music.

Emily sighed as she found the page in her book and tried to concentrate, wondering whether she really did have the guts to mention the rules, let alone reset them. He sat beside her but had no book tonight, seemed content to lie down, using her thighs as his pillow. She stroked his hair with her fingers, unable to resist touching. He turned his face towards her. She felt his warmth through her shirt. Maybe he wasn't so content because she could feel his fingers, feel his breath, feel his…lips.

He batted her book with his hand, knocking it to the floor

She shifted back a fraction and looked down.

'You weren't reading it anyway,' he defended, eyes dancing.

She leant forward this time, so her sensitive nipple brushed his mouth again. 'You were making that impossible.'

He didn't deny it, just made any kind of concentration impossible again with his teasing tongue. She sighed, eyes closing, giving in.

But he stopped, smiled once more when she looked at him. 'I have something for you.' He reached a hand under the sofa and pulled out a small rectangular box.

She looked at it and marvelled at how fast her heart could suddenly beat without warning. She knew that brand—the world-famous jewellery store. She told herself to calm down—it wasn't the shape of a ring box—besides, she didn't want any kind of box, she wanted… 'Luca—'

'Open it.'

It took a little more effort than she'd thought it would. When it finally clicked, she stared at the contents. Confusion blinded her. On the backdrop of velvet so navy it was almost black rested the most exquisite bracelet she'd ever seen. It was fine and, oh, how it sparkled, even like that, lying still in the box. Diamond after diamond after diamond, strung together by delicate platinum.

Her heart totally stopped then. What was he doing giving her something like this? She munched the inside of her cheek. What was this for? 'Luca?'

Lying there, looking up into her face, he must have read her unease. 'Don't worry. It wasn't expensive.'

Yeah, right. 'Don't lie to me, Luca.' She shifted the box and met his eyes. 'Not even to be nice.'

He met her gaze square on. 'It wasn't expensive for me. It's just a trinket.'

It wasn't just anything, not to Emily. Questions crowded her head once more. Increasingly nasty questions. Was this part of his usual game plan? Did he buy all his lovers a beautiful piece of jewellery? Was this a little nothing, a bonbon to sweeten the goodbye? Had he bought it himself or got his secretary to race out? Or did he have a stash of them even, in a drawer in his secret bedroom that was as out of bounds as Bluebeard's dungeon? The evil thoughts kept coming, swirling before her and clouding her vision of what was a beautiful bracelet. So classical, elegant and stunning— *nothing* like her.

'Why?' It was the only word she could get out.

He sat up, leaving her lap cold. 'Because I wanted to.'

That simple, huh? *Because he wanted.* That was the way Luca liked to operate—keeping things on a simple plane.

'Why did you want to?' She really, really wanted to understand.

'I just did.' He shrugged. 'You deserve spoiling.'

'What makes you think that?'

'Oh, come on, Emily, it hasn't been easy for you these last few years.'

Her blood chilled. 'Is this about pity, Luca?'

'No. You know it isn't.'

'So what is it, then?'

'I don't know.' He frowned. 'I feel like you've earned it.'

'Earned it *how* exactly?' As his lover? Her blood was ice now and any moment she'd snap.

Silence thickened as she stared at him. He was just as relentless about staring back and his jaw grew ever more square and hard.

Finally he shook his head slowly at her. 'Why do we have to have this in-depth examination of "why"? I just wanted to give you something nice. Get you something nice. I thought it would look pretty. You have the most lovely long arms. Nice wrists.'

Now he was getting frustrated and, despite a film of reservation still keeping her cool, she couldn't stop her small smile. 'Nice wrists?'

'Yes.' His hand encircled one. 'Very fine.'

She looked back at the box to hide her see-sawing emotions. 'Thank you.'

Part of her was thrilled, flattered, flushed…but deeper inside she doubted. Despite its undeniably hefty price tag, it made her feel cheap. Baubles were not what she wanted from Luca. She'd rather have had nothing at all. One moment he was insisting on this being a stringless fling and then he was giving her this? She didn't need mixed messages and he'd just ripped the scab off her vulnerability. Because there was a wound—underneath she'd begun to want more. Words, meaning…and emotion.

Trying to hide that fact, even from herself, she turned into him, breathed in his scent, nuzzled his warm neck, and sought the response that *was* always readily given. The box slipped to the floor as she moved to get closer to him. She silenced herself with the press of her lips to his skin.

Hours later she lay awake but pretended to be asleep. She could feel the restlessness that he was trying to contain. He moved slowly but she felt the bed lift as his weight was removed from it. Felt the brief blast of cooler air as he raised the covers to escape. Now he tucked them back around her. She kept her eyes closed, trying to keep her expression relaxed as if in deep repose, for she knew that the chink in the curtains let in light from the streetlamps and he'd be able to see enough of her features to know.

But she must have done OK because he said nothing, suspected nothing, ran a finger very lightly over her shoulder and then left the room.

The first night he'd said he had to go and do some work. The second night, he'd said he had to check his email. Now he offered no excuse.

At some point *every* night, he left. He didn't want to wake next to her, to start the day with her at his side. It only underlined the level of their relationship—that there wasn't one. And while that was what they'd agreed to, Emily knew it wasn't what she wanted any more.

CHAPTER EIGHT

LUCA appeared only a couple of hours after leaving for work again. Emily was alone at the piano.

'Your friend Pascal phoned.' She stopped playing as soon as she realised he was quietly coming over to her. 'He said he was looking forward to catching up with you tonight at dinner and that he hoped Micaela wasn't on maternity leave yet.'

He halted, halfway across the floor. 'You answered the phone?'

'Yes.' Brows lifted, she matched his hard look.

'Why didn't you let Micaela answer it?'

'Micaela wasn't here,' she replied with care. 'It was just before she arrived.'

'Why did you answer it? Why didn't you just let it ring?'

'Because when phones ring it's normal to answer them. Because it might have been a temp agency. Do I even need a because?' Her hackles snapped up. 'So I answered the phone. I'm so sorry. Was that not on my list of allowable activities?' She shut the lid of the piano. 'Perhaps you'd better write down a list of "dos and don'ts" for me.' She barely paused for breath, realising that her time to renegotiate the rules was right *now*. 'What should I do if someone comes to the door—go hide in the wardrobe?'

He jerked a step away. 'Emily, don't be ridiculous.'

'I'm not. I'm happy to be a holiday fling, but I'm not going to hide away like some sort of secret lover.'

'I don't—'

'If you want a private plaything why not just get an inflatable doll?'

'A doll wouldn't do those sexy sighs the way you do.' He turned his back, about to exit. 'I'll call Pascal and cancel.'

'Why?' Suspicious. There had been such personality in the brief exchange she'd had with the man and she had to admit she was half dying to meet someone Luca dealt with on a personal level rather than an employment one. Until this call she'd been beginning to wonder if there was *anyone* Luca dealt with on a personal level. 'Because I'm here?'

He swung back, looked uncomfortable. 'I have a reputation to maintain.'

What reputation? And how the hell was she going to damage it? 'What's wrong with having a girlfriend?' She saw she'd picked the wrong word in the way he froze. 'A lover,' she immediately rephrased. 'Why do I even have to be defined?' She rapidly changed tack again. 'Aren't I just someone you're helping out for a few days?'

'Because the dinner is business. I keep business and personal separate.'

So he didn't want to introduce her to anyone. 'That's rubbish. That's just a pathetic excuse for not building any kind of a relationship with your current lover—other than in bed.' And she didn't believe this dinner was all business—why would Pascal phone so early at Luca's house if it were? Why would he know about Micaela and her baby? Wouldn't he just leave a message with Luca's secretary at work? 'Am I really not fit for display? Not good enough to mix with your friends and associates?'

Only good enough to sleep with? Did he think all he had to do was toss a few diamonds her way to keep her happy?

'Of course you are.' Luca's face had flushed. 'But I don't usually have women staying here.'

'Well, I can move out. Shall I go put up at the B & B down the road? I could earn my crust making beds there.'

'Don't be ridiculous.'

'Well, it's either make theirs, or perform in yours.'

Now he looked really angry. 'You are the one used to making money on the street.'

She nodded. 'And you're the one treating me like a whore.'

'I am not and you know it.'

'No, I don't. Have your damn dinner party. I'm quite happy to go back to the hostel.' She picked up her cardigan, intending a snappy exit. 'Go screw yourself, Luca.'

He grabbed her arm, ripped the cardy from her fingers and flung it back across the room. 'No! You don't say something like that and think you can walk away from it,' he yelled. 'What the hell do you want from me?'

'I don't know!' she yelled right back. 'But I'll tell you what I don't want. I don't want your money. I don't want *things* from you.'

'Is this about that bracelet? OK, fine. I'll never buy you anything else because it was so damn awful of me. So what's left, Emily?'

'You tell me.'

'I have nothing more to give. You know this. A good time. That's all.'

'A good time is more than just sex. You could give me some respect too. Some *time*.'

'I do have to work, Emily.'

'Twenty hours a day?'

'Usually, yes. But not this week, in case you haven't noticed. I've been home in the middle of the damn day.'

'And for what exactly? A tumble in bed?'

'No-holds-barred sex and nothing else. *Your* idea.'

'The complete holiday package. *Your* idea.'

'What, you're saying the onboard entertainment officer needs to lift his game, that it?'

'Absolutely.' Vexed, wanting to hide the hurt, she rolled her eyes and turned away. 'I shouldn't stay here. I should go.'

There was a long silence.

'Maybe you should,' he said softly. 'But you can't, can you?'

'No,' she admitted. 'Because, fool that I am, I still want you. I find it very difficult to say no to you. You look at me with those eyes, ask me with that voice and while my brain says one thing my mouth says another. Temptation, Luca.' She looked at him. 'You embody it.'

Brooding, almost black eyes dominated his face. 'So do you, Emily.' And then the smallest of smiles pulled his lips.

'I think it's good to take up temptation's offer now and
then. The chance doesn't happen all that often.'

Not for her, no, but for him it must all the time. He was
exceptionally attractive and there must be a list of women
a mile long who'd like to be in her shoes right now. She
hated the whole imaginary lot of them.

He sighed. 'I'd forgotten the dinner party. I'll go and tell
Micaela now.'

Emily, smarting with insecurity, with the uncomfortable
feeling that she'd had to force this little from him, saw a
chance to strike back. 'You're going to land a dinner party
on her at this late hour?'

He gave her a sideways look. 'Micaela is well used to
catering for me. She's completely capable.'

'You're expecting her to serve for you?'

'Of course. That's her job.'

'What about Marco?'

'What about him?' Luca looked mystified.

'Who'll look after him?'

'Ricardo, of course. The child does have a father. Or
don't you think fathers are capable of looking after their
offspring?'

Not all fathers, no. She winced. His hand lifted, a quick
frown tightened his features, but she got in before he could
open that can of worms any further.

'I'm sure he's perfectly capable, but I imagine you'll
have him off doing some other urgent business,' she blus-
tered.

'Well, I'm not going to get him to drain the pool tonight,
Emily,' he said witheringly. 'Look, Micaela and Ricardo

have been working for me for years. I pay well above the standard rate and we're all happy. I don't think it's something you need to worry about.'

'Well, have you watched her trying to iron your damn sheets recently?'

'What?' At his stunned look she knew she had him.

'Ironing your sheets. Of all the things—I mean, what sort of la-de-da request is that, oh, lord and master? The woman is swamped in them. What are they—king-size plus?'

'Ironing my sheets?'

Emily nodded curtly as if it were the crime of the century. 'Mountains of the things and she's *so* pregnant.'

'You're right,' he said briskly. 'It's a waste of time, especially while I have you around to rumple them anyway. I'll take them off her list of "dos and don'ts".' Sarcasm all the way.

The victory was bitter and not nearly enough—they weren't his sheets she was rumpling, were they? Not the ones on his bed in his private lair. And his arrogant assumption that she'd still be around to rumple them—even though she would—made her all the more irrationally angry. All the more determined to score a decent point.

'You might own everything in sight, Luca, but that doesn't give you the right to be so arrogant. Is this why you got divorced? Your wife couldn't be bothered putting up with your attitude any more?'

'I'm not divorced.'

'What?'

He'd gone glacial, repeated the words slow and cold. 'I'm not divorced.'

She stared at him. Not divorced? There was a wife somewhere? Harsh, sick anger rose in her chest—acrid, stinging bile burning its way up.

No wonder he didn't want people knowing she was here. No wonder he didn't want her sleeping in his own bed—her scent mixing with that of his absent wife? What, was she on holiday somewhere? Fury clouded her judgment, her logic.

She swore she saw guilt wisp across his face before the heat of anger chased it away. What had happened? Had she left him? He left her? Emily lost it at the thought of his infidelity—her every cell screamed in denial. Even though she knew he must have…he must…

Rage turned everything red. She opened her mouth to hurl the venom at him but he, as visibly irate as she, got in first.

'She *died*.' His lips barely moved as he ground out the answer.

It was a full minute before she moved. Even longer for him—rigid with the effort of containing high-running emotion.

Finally, Emily released a painful breath. Remorse, pity, despair exploded inside. Her eyes, her nose, stung as if she'd sucked in some poisonous gas.

'Luca…' Her voice caught. 'I'm so sorry.' Not just for his loss, but for her thoughts of just a few seconds ago—thoughts that she knew had been written all over her face. 'Why didn't you tell me?'

'Why would I?'

She flinched. That one hurt. Hard and unforgiving and

a bitter reminder of her *nothing* status. Her vision fogged as she turned away. She heard him swear under his breath.

'Emily—'

'No, you're right,' she gabbled, walking to the door. 'It's none of my business.'

'I'm sorry I snapped.' He grabbed her arm. 'I didn't mean that.' He held on hard and she had to stop walking. 'It's just that it was a really long time ago and I don't like to think about it much. Or talk about it. Or anything. Much.'

She blinked. 'I'm sorry too.' She couldn't look at him. 'I shouldn't have been so rude.'

'Stay here. I'll just have a word to Micaela.'

He stood just outside the door and called to Micaela. They yabbered for a few minutes; Emily understood nothing of what they said. But she understood so much more of him now: why he held her, and the rest of the world, at a distance. Not only had he buried his wife. He'd buried his heart with her.

He reappeared in the doorway. 'Dinner will be at eight.'

'I'm not going to be here, Luca.'

'Yes, you are.' He crossed the room and infiltrated her space enough to send her pulse crazy. Damn, rational thought was impossible when all the oxygen seemed to be sucked away in his presence. 'We're not done yet and you know it. You just admitted it. Besides—' he inhaled deeply and seemed to force more lightness in his tone '—you'd be doing me a favour. In fact I'd really appreciate your company.'

'Why?' What was with this complete, and obviously concerted, change of heart?

'There are a couple of people coming tonight. Pascal, who you spoke to, I've known for ages. He was my mentor—has a formidable knowledge of the markets and taught me everything. He's also been happily married for the last fifty years. He wants the same for me and has taken it upon himself to find me a replacement wife. He always brings a possible candidate to dinner. This current one is a consultant with the London branch of his company. He's brought her the last couple of times we've met up. Having you there will be a good shield.'

'You want me to—'

'Protect me from the unwanted advances of another woman—yes.' His mouth made the movements of a smile but there was too much of an edge.

'That's ridiculous.' It was ridiculous. As if he'd ever need that. He certainly didn't want a replacement wife. He couldn't have made that clearer to Emily, but that was the point, wasn't it? She was his shield from another woman trying to get close and she was good protection because she already knew her place.

Suddenly she had no desire whatsoever to protect him now. She was hurt and she wanted him to open right up. And while he'd changed his mind about tonight, she didn't have the lack of interest or the dignity to refuse—she wanted to know more before she left. She wanted to know everything. What had happened to his wife? How long was a long time ago? And what was this woman coming tonight like? Why did his old mentor think she'd be a good match for him? Emily's emotions were all at sea and jealousy was the next to fly its flag.

'Have you slept with her?' She made no apology for the rudeness of her question. She just had to know.

'No.' His lips went firm.

'Do you want to?'

'No.'

Uh-huh. Consultants were bound to be beautiful and slim and well maintained as well as brilliant and she refused to believe the woman wouldn't be interested in Luca. There wasn't a woman alive who wouldn't be interested in Luca.

His temper flashed again. 'If I'd wanted to, I would have by now.'

By now she'd thought enough to be able to believe him. He was so determined to compartmentalise his life and he'd be too disciplined to blur the lines. Too hurt by the past?

He bent, glaring right in her eyes, and still felt the need to raise his voice and fire the words in her face. 'This is the thing, Emily—I don't screw around and I don't cheat.' His jaw was tight. 'Eight p.m. Here. Wear something half-decent.'

Emily recoiled at the blunt instruction. It was as if he'd slapped her across the cheek and all her sympathy sank under the force of it. So he did think she'd embarrass him. Did she have no manners? No class? No decent clothes, obviously. And he didn't take her out because she wasn't good enough to be seen with.

For a second he stared at her, a beat of amazement in his eyes, before his frustration blew. A short, sharp, crude oath and he was gone. Three seconds later the house shook as the front door slammed.

CHAPTER NINE

EMILY counted to twenty and then went in search of grissini. She needed something she could snap her teeth on—to crunch away her anger and grind away her guilt, because right now she felt bucket-loads of both.

In the kitchen, Micaela was at the bench, restraint tightening her usually friendly face. As Emily went into the pantry she wondered just how much of that argument she'd heard. Heat scorched her cheeks. So yesterday she and Luca had been at it like rabbits mid-morning, and today they were yelling at each other. It couldn't make for a pleasant working environment. But Micaela was busy making meal preparations and not looking her in the eye.

'Where's Marco?' Another awful thought occurred to her—was the poor kid hiding in his cupboard under the stairs?

'He's at a neighbour's playing today.'

Emily released another difficult breath, glad that he hadn't been around to overhear them fighting. 'I'm sorry if...I...er...'

Micaela put down the knife she was scoring tomatoes

with and turned briskly to face her. 'I want to tell you something. It is personal and I hope you don't mind but I want to tell you.' It was as if she'd been putting the words together in her head for the last five minutes and finally decided to launch forth.

Her grissini suspended mid-air, Emily wondered what the hell it was all about.

'It's difficult for us to get pregnant. We tried and tried for so long. But nothing. Then we found out that we needed help.'

Emily blinked. She didn't know what she'd expected but it wasn't that.

'My family is all in Italy. We didn't have much money and we had no one to turn to.'

Turn to for what? Emily couldn't keep up with the speed of the subject.

Micaela's eyes were dark and shiny and emotion wobbled her voice. 'Luca gave us Marco and he gave us this baby.'

And for one moment, one awful, jealousy-ridden, rottenly hideous moment, Emily thought Micaela meant that Luca had fathered her children.

'He gave us the money.'

Emily put the grissini down and sagged back against the bench. What was it with her and wrong conclusions today?

'For treatment. For doctors.'

Thank heavens Micaela didn't seem to have noticed her almost collapse, too busy getting all the details out.

'We've been going to a private clinic for years. Thousands and thousands of pounds for treatment so we could try and try again—for as long as we wanted to. He said there was no limit. That it was up to us.' She picked up the knife again, head bent as she sliced into the tomato. 'He told us it was part of our health-insurance package as our employer. But it is directly from him.'

She directed a piercing gaze at Emily then, and all her caring and gratitude was evident in the way her eyes were watering and the fierce way she spoke. 'He works too hard. He is too hard on himself. He is a good man. And he deserves...'

'What?' Emily prompted. No wonder they were so loyal to their employer, so happy to drop everything and come running when summoned. No wonder she ironed his damn sheets.

'He deserves to be happy.'

Emily closed her eyes. Yes, he did. But didn't everyone? Didn't she too?

'He should have the kind of happiness he's given Ricardo and me.'

Love. Children. A family.

Now Emily felt worse, because it seemed that Luca had almost had that, only to lose it, and now he didn't want it at all. And she, not realising, had taunted him.

She wished he'd told her before. She'd told him about her parents. But he'd had no intention of ever getting to know Emily well enough to have to bother. Only she'd made him. She rolled the breadstick back and forth on the bench. Thought about what Micaela had told her and why she had told her—because she wanted her to see the best of Luca? 'How long have you worked for him?'

'Almost eight years. He said I should stop when I got pregnant, but I like working. It keeps my mind off worrying.'

Emily understood. Wasn't that what she'd done back home—kept herself busy as a way of burying her fears? And now her lips burned with questions about Luca's past. But she couldn't ask them. It would be prying and Micaela probably wouldn't tell her anything anyway. She'd share her own personal story, but not that of her employer. Her loyalty was too strong and rightly so. Emily didn't want to make her uncomfortable. Besides, she'd rather hear about it from Luca himself.

He was such a challenge to her—and now, with the mention of this woman tonight, she felt a streak of competitiveness too. She'd show him, and all of them, just how damn stylish she could be...

But something 'half decent'? Her pack was filled with lightweight trousers and skirts and old tee shirts. Her wardrobe hadn't been the priority for some time—like, ever. It was Kate who'd had her hair done, who had the fashionable clothes—as the singer centre stage she'd needed to. Emily, the accompanist, had only needed a black top and trousers so she wouldn't stick out.

She looked at Micaela, at the way the Italian was still chic and gorgeous despite having a belly the size of an award-winning watermelon. Emily needed her kind of help. 'Can you recommend a shop that sells nice clothes that aren't too expensive? One that might have something suitable to wear to a dinner party?'

Micaela, her self-possession fully restored, sent her a

broad smile. She didn't just give her the name of the place, she drew her a map.

Luca pushed back from his desk and took a turn around the room. Guilt licked his feet like the burning flames of a small fire that he'd accidentally stumbled on barefoot. Impatiently he moved, trying to stamp out the unpleasant sensation. Adding to that discomfort, irritation whipped at his back. He didn't want to do dinner parties. He didn't want to go out and be social. He just wanted to stay home and be with Emily. The only thing salving the annoyance was the fact that she'd admitted she couldn't leave him yet. Good, because he couldn't let her go.

He wasn't angry because she'd made him think about Nikki, but because she'd so obviously thought the worst of him. But then, why shouldn't she? He'd underlined the temporary, nothing-more-to-it-than-the-physical nature of their affair—of course she probably thought he did it all the time like some cheating stud out for cheap thrills… But her judgment hurt. *What she thought of him mattered*—and that was the real problem.

He paused at the corner of his office where the sheets of glass met, giving a spectacular view over the city. Pascal was the problem too. If it had been anyone else who had called, that argument wouldn't have happened. But for Pascal and Emily to meet? Luca felt so uncomfortable about that.

But he had to host him—Pascal rarely came to London now. Part of him wanted to—but that part was small compared to the part that wanted another night with Emily all to himself. Guilt took another bite. The old man had done so much for him. He owed him. And even though Pascal had insisted that he wanted to see him settled, it wasn't that black and white. He had been there when Nikki died. He was the one person who knew it all. They almost never spoke of it, but that didn't mean it wasn't there.

He walked home—cutting it fine time wise—stopped in the kitchen first off to check if Micaela was holding up OK. He'd had no idea she ironed his sheets—teased her about it and told her to stop. She smiled and waved him away. He breathed deep and savoured the aromas. Of course she'd have it in hand. Emily had that one so far wrong. He paid the couple more than three times the going rate, but only because they were worth it. They were loyal and hard-working and, yes, went the extra mile when he needed them to. Which wasn't anywhere near as often as Emily might think—certainly not since Micaela had got pregnant.

He didn't go in search of Emily, not concerned that she might have moved out after the row that morning. He'd instructed Micaela days ago to let him know if she made any sign of leaving for good. And some more breathing time after this morning wouldn't go astray. He showered and dressed, tucking in his shirt as he walked back down to her room.

He knocked and went straight in. He took one look at her and was glad he'd taken those extra moments to breathe because there was no air getting to his lungs now. They'd shut down. So had everything else in his body, save one organ south of his belt. And then his heart started pounding.

It was just a black dress. Not even that revealing. But those arms and legs were on show, a slight hint of the deep cleavage, and a lot of back. That meant…he fought to focus…

'You're not wearing a bra.'

'Hello to you too.' She turned and gave him a cool look. 'No, I'm not. Is that not decent enough for you?'

When he'd told her to wear something half decent, he hadn't meant dressy. He'd meant something to cover her up. She was all bare arms and legs all the time and he didn't want to be a total picture of distraction when Pascal was here. Like a dog salivating over a particularly juicy piece of meat.

It hadn't come out right, but he'd been too rattled to rephrase. He'd seen the spark in her eye, known he'd scored a hit—not one he'd meant, but at the time he'd felt a gleam of misplaced satisfaction because it had felt as if she was knocking at him left, right and centre. And then he'd just felt wildly angry with her, with himself and with the whole damn uncontrolled mess. But clearly she'd taken it to heart because the woman before him now was the epitome of sultry sophistication.

She turned back to the mirror, lifted her strawberry-blonde hair and twisted it up. He was sorry; he loved the length of it, the depth of colour, wanted to run his fingers into it. Only now, as she secured it with a few clips, her cheekbones were displayed. And the odd strand feathered down, wisping around her ear, her neck, and he wanted to kiss the parts of her they pointed to.

He cleared his throat, looked away. Not tonight—at least, not now. He braced every muscle, determined to calm his raging hormones. He only had to get through a few hours. That was all. He could manage that, couldn't he?

CHAPTER TEN

EMILY concentrated on applying her mascara, trying to apply a brake to the mad acceleration of her heart. Luca crossed the room and picked up the box she'd placed on the table—she hadn't been sure what she'd wanted to do with it.

The diamonds caught the light as he lifted the bracelet out. He walked towards her, holding the chain out straight. 'Wear it for me.'

She met his eyes; the fire burned in them, melting that hard chocolate.

'OK.' It wasn't about the bracelet, it was about him. And she couldn't say no.

He wound it round her wrist and did the clasp. The metal was cold at first but soon warmed against her skin. Glancing back in the mirror, she pushed another pin into her loose topknot and as she did the bracelet slid down her arm a little, catching the light again and sparkling brilliantly. It was beautiful. No other adornment would ever be necessary. It lifted her simple black dress into something stunning and it lifted her status into something nearer his—she couldn't be confused with the waiting staff now. Part of her loved it—how could she not? And yet part of her hated it—and the soulless contract she felt it represented. Was he worried about tonight and how she was going to come across? Was he sprucing her up with an expensive piece of jewellery?

'Am I decent now?' she asked softly.

As she waited she saw his tension increasing, but it wasn't a flush of desire growing; if anything he'd gone paler beneath his brown tan and his body was tense. 'When I asked you to wear—'

'Asked? It was more of an order, Luca.'

'Whatever. I didn't mean dressy. Your arms, your legs poke out from those tee shirts and they tempt me. And now…' His jaw clamped, as if he was holding back more.

'Now what?'

'There's your back. And there's no bra. And you're too beautiful.'

She squared her shoulders. 'Do you want me to change?'

'No.'

She tilted her chin and decided to play with that one advantage she did have.

'Don't look at me like that, Emily.'

'Like what?' OK, so in her mind she was removing his clothes, piece by piece.

'Emily…' He sounded half-strangled.

She ran her hands from his shoulders to his waist. 'You look good too.'

Good enough to eat. She stood on tiptoe so she could press her mouth to his. Only she didn't, instead she took only his lower lip, sucking it into her mouth and then catching it between her teeth to give it a nip, then sucking again. Oh, yes, he was definitely good enough to eat.

He stood frozen, so she did it again, stepping in closer to invade all his space.

His hands smoothed over the curve of her bottom, and as her teeth nipped the second time his fingers curled into her softness and he pulled her right into his hips.

She smiled as she felt his body harden. *This* was the tension she liked to see in him. She held his jaw in her hands, fingers fluttering over the freshly shaved skin, and kissed him some more, teased him some more, tortured him some more. And he, rock-hard, let her. Until he groaned and his hands pushed while his pelvis thrust. One hand went to her dress, lifting the hem.

It was the sound of the door opening downstairs that stopped her. She listened to Micaela greeting the guests, then whispered, 'We can't. They've arrived.'

'We can,' he growled, breathing harsh, grinding his hips against hers. 'They'll wait.'

'You are so arrogant. We *can't* be rude. They're here already.'

'We can. We only need ten, twenty seconds, tops.'

She laughed against his lips. 'Not enough.'

Groaning, he pushed her away. 'Damn it, it'll take me longer to calm down than it would have to follow through on that.'

Giggling, she did a final fuss in the mirror for damage control.

'It's not funny.' He turned his back on her and stalked to the door. She followed him down to the foyer, watching from a distance as he pressed a kiss on the woman's cheek, shook the hand of the older man.

'What's that perfume you're wearing, Luca? So lovely and floral.' She was as stylish as to be expected. Slim, sophisticated and coyly sharp. 'It really suits you.'

Pascal's sharp eyes flew from Luca's slightly forced smile to Emily's own on-fire face. Emily saw him swap a smile of amusement with the woman and was confused. Surely if Pascal wanted Luca and her to get together he wouldn't be looking so pleasantly surprised about Emily's presence? And as for the unsubtle question mark hanging over her involvement with him…

But Luca was downplaying it. 'Francine, Pascal, meet Emily. She's a friend who's just arrived from New Zealand.'

Unfortunately, the way he was avoiding her eyes pretty much denied the 'friend' status, but Pascal and Francine both smiled and said hello. Emily managed to murmur a similar response.

'How's Madeline?' Luca asked.

'Beautiful as ever,' Pascal replied. 'She sends her love.'

Luca nodded. 'Come through. Micaela has been slaving all afternoon just for you.'

He sent Emily a look then. She refused to bite at it, after all, if she were Micaela, she'd slave too. They went straight to the intimate table in the dining room and caught up on news as their appetiser was served. It seemed Francine was soon heading off to a business school just outside Paris.

'You were at Oxford, weren't you, Luca?' Francine asked.

'For my undergraduate degree, yes, but post-graduate was Harvard.'

Of course. He was elite all over whereas Emily was…

Francine turned to her. 'Where did you study, Emily?'

'I didn't,' she answered, battling the inferior feeling and failing. 'I left school and went straight into work. Retail.'

'Retail?' Francine-the-sophisticated delicately speared a piece of tomato with her fork.

Oh, God, this was a nightmare.

'Yes, you know, a shop assistant. Standing on your feet for hours, dusting, displaying stock, that sort of thing.'

She sensed Luca's posture tighten. What, shouldn't she admit to her working-class history?

'Oh.' Francine brightened. 'I like shopping. What was your speciality? Fashion? Perfume?'

'Sadly no.' Emily smiled sweetly. 'At first it was the hardware department of a bargain outlet store. Cheap power tools, drill bits and gardening implements. Then I moved around departments—footwear, toys, furniture… and I worked in a CD and DVD store at night.'

There, she'd let them know it. She was nothing on their education, their sophistication, their elitism. But she was all about hard work, and prioritising and getting things done. She'd had to. Three loads of washing on before she left the house, making Kate's lunch, leaving something for her father. Racing home to get the washing in off the line in her lunch break and get the next load out there, all the while having dinner slowly cooking in a crockpot. She'd had it all mastered. For years she'd done it all. And now, when she was finally free of it, she felt so empty and so vacant and so out of place.

Pascal was chuckling, but with a kindly twinkle. 'A DVD store? You must know your movies.'

'And music, yes.'

'I love movies.' Francine smiled. 'What's your favourite ever?'

Emily blinked. She hadn't expected them to accept her bald recitation of her utter averageness—or actually be interested.

'If you could have studied, what subject would it have been?' Pascal asked, seeming to understand that it was because she hadn't been able to, not because she had chosen not to.

Emily let a genuine smile out then and decided to sharpen up her act. She'd been verging on rude and that wasn't her. Her defence mechanism was set unnecessarily on high. 'Music and movies, I guess.'

They laughed and fractionally the atmosphere lightened. They discussed the current films on release—half of which Emily had seen on the plane over. She would have relaxed, settled into the swing of it, but for the ominously quiet presence on the other side of her. Each time she glanced in his direction she encountered the frown in his eyes, it made her too adrenalin-charged and aware to truly enjoy the conversation.

She forced attention onto the beautiful Francine—asking her about her upcoming MBA course and then about city life in London. Which shops were the best, which were the tourist spots she shouldn't fail to see...

Francine's coy look resurfaced at that. 'Surely Luca is showing you the best on offer?'

She couldn't have known the significance those words would have. *The best.* Emily turned to look at Luca then, staring him out as he lifted his glass and took more than a decent sip of wine.

'He's trying, I guess,' Emily answered calmly, 'but some things he just doesn't have a clue about.'

His eyes flashed at hers and she felt his knee under the table, pressing hard into hers. A warning if ever there was one.

'Don't worry, Luca.' Pascal laughed. 'You can't be brilliant at everything.'

She could feel his fire crackling. After that she resorted to not looking in his direction at all. She carried the conversation completely with Francine and Pascal while he sat, the almost-silent observer.

Micaela served dessert and Luca insisted she then head home.

'I hope you like it.' Micaela smiled as she said goodbye, but it seemed the smile was directed most pointedly at Emily.

Wondering why, Emily glanced into the bowl. It was the creamy confection that Luca had spooned into her that day in the Giardino.

Emily paused, spoon in hand. Not sure she wanted to taste it again for fear it wouldn't be as sublime as it had been that day. Not wanting to ruin the memory.

'Try it, Emily.' It was the first time he'd addressed her directly all evening and she knew then that he'd ordered it specially.

Just as she lifted the spoon to her lips she felt his hand. Startled, she glanced at him. He held his spoon with his left hand, while it appeared his other rested on his knee beneath the table. But it was on her thigh that his fingers sat. And as she tasted the sweet his fingers slid over the material of her dress, up and down the length of her thigh. She sent him an agonised look but he had his head turned and was talking to Francine.

The pudding was divine—and so was the orgasmic fantasy of sharing it with Luca…on Luca…all over…

She put her spoon down, unable to eat anything more. Barely controlling the urge to part her legs and let his fingers slip all the way up. What was he trying to do to her?

At last the others finished and Emily was glad to be able to scoop up their empty dishes and take them into the kitchen. She insisted the others remain at the table. She needed a breather—not from the guests but from the intensity of Luca, from the pent-up passion she could feel in him and the response he was seeking from her. But as she placed the plates down she heard footsteps behind her in the kitchen and he whispered her name. She turned but he caught her, pulling her backwards into his embrace, lifting her back behind the door. His mouth was hot on the side of her neck—kissing and sucking. His hands were everywhere. She leant back against him, and like kerosene-drenched wood their passion ignited into an inferno.

'Luca?'

He said nothing but kissed her even more fiercely. His hands slid up her bare thighs, lifting under her dress and up to her knickers. But he didn't slide his fingers inside them as she wanted him to. She arched back in invitation. Oh, she wanted everything. Control of the urges suspended between them for hours snapped at the first touch. There was anger and hurt and most of all need.

She forgot everything—where she was, what she was supposed to be doing. All she could think of was Luca and how he felt and how badly she wanted him back deep inside—then it would all be right, right, *right*.

The tips of his fingers stroked over the lace and silk. Close, so close and yet not touching her heat as hard as she needed. His other hand cupped her breast. His thumb worked back and forth over her tight, jutting nipple. And from behind he rubbed against her, pressing his erection against her rounded, hungry flesh.

Sandwiched between his fingers and his aroused pelvis she rocked, seeking satisfaction from both. Wanting the barriers of their clothing gone so she could feel everything fresh and raw.

'Do you want me, Emily?' he muttered, mouth hard against her neck.

'Yes.'

'Shall I bend you over that bench and just—?'

'Oh, yes…' she panted, knees buckling. 'Now. Now!' She was so close she'd climax as soon as he thrust in—she knew it and she wanted it. As hard and fast and as animal as he liked. She couldn't fight her hunger any more, couldn't fight him.

But his hands left her body. He stepped away so fast she staggered—his hands came back again, steadying her.

'Emily,' he panted, more breathless than she'd ever heard him. 'You're right. We can't.'

'What are you doing?'

'Torturing us both.'

'Why?'

He didn't answer directly. She felt his head resting on her shoulder, but he held the rest of him away from her. 'I want you like I have never wanted before.'

There it was again—want. And there was an unmistakable note of agony in there as well. She closed her eyes. He didn't want to want her like this.

'I'd better get back to the others.' He pulled away.

'I need a minute.'

'Of course.' He took another couple of deep breaths and left.

She made it to the bathroom but there was no way she could disguise the colour in her cheeks or the redness of her mouth. It had only been minutes—maybe three? But everything had changed.

CHAPTER ELEVEN

LUCA watched her walk into the lounge. Head high, cheeks flushed. He could almost hear the thunder as the lightning look flashed from her eyes—on fire and unforgiving. It wasn't missed by the others either in a moment of utter silence.

She went to the piano.

'Do you play, Emily?' Francine asked.

'A little.'

'You'll play for us now?'

She nodded. He was relieved because it meant the end of having to hear her conversation for a while and he wouldn't have to meet her eyes again either. That look made him feel worse and he already felt like a jerk. He hadn't meant for it to happen, to get so far out of control. But all through dinner he'd watched her discomfort, listened to her put herself down. He didn't give a damn about whether she'd been to uni or not—nor did the others. Didn't she understand that he knew how hard she'd worked? She'd achieved something far more important than a few choice grades at university—she'd taken on a workload and level

128 BETWEEN THE ITALIAN'S SHEETS

of responsibility many people with PhDs wouldn't cope with and she couldn't have done a better job of building her sister's confidence and independence.

But at what cost to herself? Her own life, her own ambition had been put on hold and he wanted to see her take charge of it. Just then he'd wanted to reassure her—let her know how beautiful she was, how bright, how giving—and the simplest way to do that was by showing how much he wanted her. Big mistake—once he'd touched, he'd almost lost complete control.

She played a few chords experimentally. 'I don't have the voice of my sister.'

He tensed, damn her defensive downplaying again.

'And while I love classical, I must be honest and admit I prefer a little blue with my tunes.' Her fingers slid on the keys, adjusting a note here and there and the result became a jazz standard.

Her voice was lower and had a husk to it and he was almost in a puddle. And as she hit her stride there was a raw quality he almost couldn't stand to listen to.

While she didn't have the brilliance of her sister's tone, she had a far greater emotional depth. Luca knew first hand the reservoir of feeling within Emily. It intrigued him, aroused him and scared him.

She kept it short and he was glad because he wasn't sure he could take much more—this looking but not touching was just about killing him. Then Francine asked her to play another. He gritted his teeth.

'Only if you sing this time.' Emily's huskiness was more apparent.

He shifted in his seat, recognising that she was wrung out and frustrated with his inability to do anything about it. Fortunately Francine smiled and sat beside her and did the singing and Luca watched as Emily won her over completely. And then he just watched her. The light played on the diamonds at her wrist just as he'd imagined it would. He would never regret buying her the gift. She did deserve spoiling. It was stunning, elegant and classical—just like her. And also like her, it shone bright with an internal fire. Only now he regretted that he hadn't chosen handcuffs. Then he could chain her to his bed and have her as much as he liked—and keep her from invading other areas of his life. But she was like this force barrelling into him, challenging the things in the world he'd worked hard to establish—like peace, solitude and isolation.

'You find her very beautiful.' Pascal's tone was low and Luca started.

Hell, he'd forgotten the old man was right beside him. He'd forgotten—

'You can't take your eyes off her.'

'I find her frustrating.' As was his attraction to her—uncontrollable, insatiable, undeniable. Even now, right now, he wanted her.

He turned to Pascal, blinked as he looked into those brown eyes that held understanding and just a tinge of sadness—brown eyes that were so familiar and yet for a few moments there had been forgotten. Desolation washed through him. Despair. How could he have forgotten? Guilt seized his heart and he looked quickly away. He'd tried so hard to make eyes just like those happy. And a long time ago, for a few magical moments, he'd succeeded. But then there'd been nothing and there could never be anything again.

'I'm sorry, Pascal.' Sorry for the past, sorry for tonight. Sorry for his failures both then and now. He stood, wanting to end this line of conversation before it even got started. 'Let's go out to the balcony. I'll concentrate better there.'

They could talk work and avoid the personal and Luca could try to go back to denial. But he suspected it was too late. He hadn't been able to control the way she got to him, certainly hadn't been able to hide it. And now he felt his guilt grow. He hadn't wanted to bring pain to anyone.

Pascal and Francine didn't stay late. Pascal explained that he had too much work to do in the morning before flying back to Paris. Emily had sat quietly listening for that last half hour as Luca had taken over the conversational duties and he and the others had talked money and markets and things she had no idea about. She hadn't even been able to look at Luca, had been too wobbly for words.

As Luca was helping Francine with her coat Emily found Pascal standing near her. He spoke softly. 'Don't let him stamp out your fire. It's good for him. You warm him up and he's been cold for too long.' And with that he was gone, following the beautiful Francine down the stairs. Surprised, she stared after him, not really listening as Luca said the final farewells.

The door closed and she blinked. She looked at Luca directly for the first time in hours then and found her fire far from gone. It blazed. He stood, his back to the door. His host facade dropped, leaving him looking big and moody and dangerous.

She shook her head at him, reined in her own frustration as she saw the lines of unhappiness deepening in his features. 'What are you thinking about?'

'The football.' He leaned right back against the door, his edge of sarcasm more bitter than humorous. 'Don't you know there isn't a man alive who doesn't hate that question?'

'Then there isn't a man alive who isn't a coward.' It was her turn to stare him out, waiting for more.

The hint of humour faded totally. 'I don't like feeling out of control and I'm out of control. I was out of control tonight.'

She took a step towards him. 'You once said that things beyond your control scare you. Do I scare you?'

His gaze dropped to her body as she stepped closer still. 'Yes. But I think that, given a little more time, I'll get that under control.'

'Is that what you want?'

'Yes. Just a fling, Emily, one that'll finish soon.'

She stopped walking then. How soon? Because she definitely wasn't done yet.

'Do you want to know what else I'm thinking?' He lifted away from the door.

'I'm not sure.' His honesty wasn't that great so far.

He walked towards her. 'I'm thinking about how much you've achieved, how hard you've worked. And yet you don't recognise it. You sit there and belittle your job and barely mention the reality of your life.'

'I'm not going to trot out the sob story to score sympathy points, Luca. You don't do that either.'

'No, but nor do I put myself down. Be proud of your achievements, Emily. Not many people could have managed all that you have.'

She looked down, watched his broad chest come closer. It was hard to be proud of her achievements when she compared them with those of someone like him or Francine.

He lifted his hand, gently stroked down her arm to clasp her wrist. 'Play the piano for me.'

Music—to soothe the savage breast and the tortured soul? Yes, she would play for him, play for them both.

As he followed her back to the lounge he unzipped her dress. It dropped and she walked right out of it. Embracing the passion still between them, she shimmied out of her knickers as well—naked completely now except for the diamond-encrusted chain that encircled her wrist. If it was going to finish soon, then she was determined to make the most of every moment.

She sat, fingers working over the keys, watching him as he walked round the piano.

'You could have been great.' He unbuttoned his shirt and shrugged it off.

'Maybe.' She knew it was possible. 'But at what price? Years and years of nothing but hard work, giving up so much for such a large battle. Even then the chances of making it are so slim. There were other things I wanted to do with my life.'

'Other things you *had* to do,' he argued. 'You had the option taken from you.'

'Yes,' she acknowledged. 'But what's life for if not to be shared with friends and family?'

'But to give up your own dreams.' He shook his head. 'It's wrong.'

He kicked off his shoes. 'My mother had dreams of performing, but my father decreed that no wife of his would ever work. I think it was the frustration that ate her up from the inside and the bitterness that caused the cancer. You should never give up your dreams, Emily.'

'What dreams?' she confessed. She hadn't had time for dreams, not until now. 'I've never had those sort of ambitions. I'm not after fame and fortune. Kate wants that and good luck to her. But it's not what I want.'

His hands had moved to where his trousers sat loose at his waist, and she smiled as he stripped before her.

'I don't need an audience of thousands to feel appreciated.' She was feeling appreciated well enough now.

'Just the odd four-year-old boy?'

'And the occasional naked man.' One magnificent, harder-than-rock, physically perfect man.

'But you must have some desires, Emily, something you want to do. Everyone does.'

'I guess.' She was still working that one out. Still figuring out what it was that she was happiest doing. Truth be told, aside from the good times with Luca, the happiest she'd been recently was when bashing the keys with Marco.

'You should chase it and grab it. Now you're free to.'

Free? Somehow free felt lonely to her.

He disappeared from view, underneath the piano. Then

she felt his hands at her feet, their slow slide from her ankles to her calves. Her smile returned.

'Play that song again.'

'Which one?' Her mind was slowly blanking everything except the sensations.

'The first one you played after dinner.'

'Why?'

'So I can do now what I wanted to do then.'

She began, and only a couple of chords into it he moved her, sliding her across the piano seat a little so she was clear of the pedals, and then he slid her forward, so she was right on the edge of the seat. She knew what was coming, could feel his mouth moving along the delicate flesh of her inner thighs. Teeth nipping, tongue soothing, lips lush and hungry. His hands pushed on her knees, pulling them wider apart so she was open for him.

Her fingers faltered.

'Keep playing.'

She closed her eyes, unable to deny him or herself. She was used to providing the accompaniment—but not to her own annihilation. For that was what this was. The slow destruction of her mind, her reason, her will. Everything was lost under his onslaught. He was the most sensual creature she'd ever met. And she ached for more of him.

Sweat dampened her skin; her breathing was short and sharp. His hands rose, gently massaging her breasts, thumbs teasing her nipples while his lips kissed and nuzzled. Her hands crashed down on the keys, any keys. Her fingers stretched rigid as the rest of her body went taut, poised on the edge.

The noise was loud and jarring and her cry rose even higher as he burrowed his face between her legs, licking and sucking, and his fingers played her with more skill than hers had ever brought to a piano.

She couldn't bear it any more. 'Luca!'

As she collapsed he lifted her down beside him on the floor, half under the piano. She curled her legs around his waist to maximise the depth. As he slid home she gazed up at him, unable to hide her adoration. 'I'm never going to be able to play the piano again without thinking of you and the most incredible orgasm I've ever had.'

He had ruined her for life.

'It's not over yet. What position do you want?'

'All of them,' she answered, taking everything while she could.

Luca was filled with the scent and sound of her. Her music still rang in his ears. Not the gentle harmony of the piano—he'd waited until that was replaced by the sounds from her mouth as she sighed for him, breathed, pleaded and finally came.

Intoxicating, addictive, and he couldn't get enough. He looked at her. She'd fallen asleep. Reluctantly he left her warm softness. Lifted and carried her to her room. She stirred only slightly. He stood beside the bed with her still in his arms, unable to give her up just yet.

Every night he went back to the private, solitary state of his room. He had to—to keep control of the situation. He had to stay in charge. Had to determine when it would end. Because if he didn't, one day he'd wake up and *she'd* be gone. As Nikki had. He had lost too much too soon. He couldn't go through that again, not ever.

But when he laid her down and covered her beautiful body with the sheet and soft blanket, she opened her eyes. Accusation pointed right at him.

'Why won't you stay with me?'

He straightened, said nothing.

She raised her brows.

'I can't.' But equally he couldn't ignore her demand for answers.

'Do I snore?'

He shook his head.

'Do you snore?'

'Not that I'm aware of.'

'Then what is it you're afraid of? You turn into a were-wolf in the middle of the night? You have bad breath in the morning? Dribble on the pillow?'

His breath of bitter laughter was barely audible. 'You say the most—'

'I say what I think, which is more than can be said for you.'

He sobered instantly and shot the answer out. 'I don't want to hurt you.'

'Who says you will?'

Hadn't he already? He could see it in her eyes, hear the faint plea in her voice despite the defensive bravado. 'I get up really early for my swim. I don't want to wake you.'

Her gaze was relentless as she ignored the fake excuse.

Right, so he had to be honest with her. She deserved

that. 'OK, then. I don't like sleeping the whole night with someone. It's too intimate.'

'Too intimate?' she repeated. 'Too intimate?' Her next repetition was even louder. 'This from the man who likes to…who likes to…' Her blush went from the roots of her hair all the way down.

'Yes,' he agreed. 'I do like to. But that's just sex.'

'Oh, right.' Sarcasm bristling. 'Just sex.'

He turned away so he wouldn't have to look at the confusion in her eyes. 'Don't, Emily. It is all it is.'

But he knew he was the one deluding himself. It was more. They talked, she made him laugh; she made him relax; she made him want—*other* things.

He hadn't been honest at all. It wasn't about her getting hurt. He was the one who didn't want to be hurt. Yet already he was aching.

CHAPTER TWELVE

LUCA woke early in his own room and alone. Only now, for the first time, he felt a finger of regret. Wouldn't it be nice to wake next to Emily's warmth? Then he remembered the madness of those moments in the kitchen where he'd nearly taken her fast and furious while his guests were waiting in the room next door and the finger of regret became a tonne of remorse. Shame filled him. He would never have dreamed of doing such a thing with Nikki. But then he'd never wanted Nikki in this way either—so *desperately*.

He got to work even earlier than usual. But once there just sat at his desk, spinning his chair away from the computer and staring out the window. For years now, he'd pushed the pain out of his head and got on with the job. Determined to prove himself—and hadn't he succeeded at that? He was worth millions…so why did it suddenly feel like nothing?

His thoughts arrowed back to Emily. She was the problem, everything had started to fracture when she'd appeared. This last week had been unnaturally intense—

just the two of them night after night. They were rapidly moving to a level of intimacy that he wasn't comfortable with. Too much, too soon. Wasn't that just the story of his life?

He needed to regain perspective. Maybe they needed to get out more, not be caught so tight in their own little world. If he saw her out and about more, the bubble would be bound to burst. He pulled up his calendar, at the list of events he usually chose to ignore. His ribs squeezed when he saw what was a possibility for tonight. Not ideal. He forced himself to take a controlled breath in and out and decided to do it anyway. It might remind him about what had been real and what was simply a passing fixation.

Decision made, he reached for the phone.

Emily woke to the sound of her mobile, flung somewhere in the room, ringing—over and over. Stumbling over her shoes, the bracelet sliding down her arm, she rummaged and eventually found it. 'Hello?'

'Are you awake?'

'Possibly.' Hell, it was early and she'd been awake half the night thinking about how wrong he was. This wasn't just sex—this was desperation and need. They were fighting for control and battling against surrender—not against each other but against this *thing* sucking them both under.

'Come out with me tonight.' His voice was soft.

'Now I know I'm dreaming.'

'No.' A half-laugh, half-groan. 'Come to a fund-raising ball at the Museum of Natural History.'

A *ball*? 'I can't.'

'Why not?'

'I haven't got anything to wear to a ball, Luca.' She'd barely coped with the dinner party—yes, she'd felt inferior. No way could she manage a ballroom full of those over-achieving, wealthy, beautiful types.

'Wear the dress you wore last night. That'll be fine.'

She hesitated. What was he up to? She knew how badly he wanted to beat out the flame between them. She sensed his struggle. Part of him had wanted to stay with her last night. She'd felt it in the way he'd held her so closely—the tenderness in that long moment before he'd lain her down. But he was determined to deny it whereas she wanted to understand it. And right now she couldn't deny either him or herself. 'OK.'

'I'll pick you up at seven.'

In her heart she knew already. What it was, why it was. She'd been wrong. There was such a thing as love at first sight.

The moment Micaela arrived she told her about the ball.

'What are you wearing?'

Emily shrugged helplessly. 'Just the dress from last night.'

Micaela, ever the efficient, kept loading the dishwasher. 'I have a wrap and an evening bag you can borrow if you like.'

'Really?'

'Leave everything to me.'

In the afternoon she swam, floating in the shallows,

avoiding the deep end of the pool. There was a nervous wobble despite the iron way she was clenching her stomach. She would fight for him. She would do OK.

After a long shower she found Micaela back, ready and waiting with her dress clean and pressed and an array of electrical appliances, make-up and accessories on the table. Micaela did her make-up with a far heavier hand than Emily had ever used. Emily had the suspicion she'd have to use gelignite to get it off but when she looked in the mirror it didn't look overdone at all. Instead Micaela had made her eyes seem an even deeper green, highlighting her pale skin. Then she tied up Emily's hair with the skill of a senior stylist at a first-class salon.

Emily gazed at the older woman. 'Is there nothing you can't do?'

Micaela giggled.

But Emily was deadly serious. 'I can see why he values you.'

'He deserves the best.' Micaela stood back to admire her work. 'He won't be able to take his eyes off you.'

Emily didn't linger near the lounge waiting for him to get home; instead she hid out in her room. There was a soft knock and he opened her door in the same second. Emily chomped hard on the inside of her cheek. His hair was still damp, he was freshly shaven, and the black tuxedo moulded his frame, skimmed over his strength and made him all the more enthralling.

For a moment they just stared at each other. Emotion almost swallowed her.

He lifted his back from the door and walked towards her, purpose evident in his pants. He was halfway there before the instruction from her brain to her body worked and she took a step back.

'No.' She forced her head to shake. 'You're not ruining my lipstick.'

He lurched to a halt. 'What are you trying to do, give me a heart attack?'

Something like that—if she could ever chip her way though the thick ice that his heart was packed in. 'I'm not kissing you before a dinner engagement ever again—remember what happened last night?'

His eyes sparked.

'Behave.' She'd meant it as a sassy joke but it came out too soft, too serious, too real.

'That's the thing, Emily. I don't want to behave when I'm with you.'

Their eyes met and she knew he was recalling as vividly as she how they'd misbehaved last night—how out of control they had spun so quickly. She tried to break the spell. 'Shouldn't we get going?'

'Mmm-hmm.' He didn't move.

She saw that look in his eye grow and, despite her own rush of desire, a vein of disappointment opened up. 'Don't you want to?'

Slowly the expression in his face shut down. 'Of course I do. Let's go.'

Luca listened as Emily chatted with Ricardo in the car. She was babbling. And as they pulled up in front of the mag-

nificently lit building, he saw the nervousness in her face.
Then he saw her chin tilt and her shoulders square and they
were on their way in.

'Luca, wonderful to see you.'

He said his hellos to the charity chiefs. 'This is Emily,
an acquaintance who's just arrived from New Zealand.'

The New Zealand thing did it. Before he knew it she was
deep in conversation with one of the driest old guys there
about bungee jumping of all things. Grinning, he took a sip
of his wine and settled back to watch her win them all over
with her smiling eyes and gratifyingly deep concentration
as she listened to them warble on. The group of people
around them grew as she was introduced to others.

Observing, occasionally adding in a smart comment, he
caught the glance passed between a couple of consultants
who he knew were complete sharks. For a time there, a few
years after Nikki had gone, a few years before now, he'd
competed in that after-hours game of drinking and excess
and women. Removed his ring and worked hard, played
hard. It was an unfulfilling phase that hadn't lasted long
and now he concentrated on winning in the business arena
alone. But he saw them edge closer, that look in their eyes.
Emily was not a toy for them to play with. And at their
predatory prowl, his possessiveness was unmasked. He
drew her away from the crowd, closer to him.

'What…?' Her words died away as she met his gaze.
Who knew what she saw there but colour ran under her skin.

'Dance with me.' He curled his arm around her. As he
escorted her to the dance floor he pulled her even closer,
took advantage of the slow song to pull her closer still.

Her flush remained, but her brows lifted. 'I thought I was just an acquaintance.'

'It didn't seem polite to add "who I sleep with at every possible opportunity".'

She giggled and they settled into the groove.

'You were nervous about tonight,' he said after a few moments.

'A little.'

'Why?'

She shrugged. 'I'm not very sophisticated or polished. These people all are.'

'You do more than hold your own with them.' Her eyes dropped from his and he gave her a gentle shake. 'You do. You're more genuine, more generous than most of the people in this room. They might have money to give, but you give more of yourself.' He badly wanted her to believe in her own gifts. 'You're a good listener, you're kind, you're funny and you're gorgeous. You had old Thomas all pink and flustered.'

She was all pink now—not from desire but from pleasure. Almost shy, her small smile was sweet. But it was the look in her eyes that really got to him—the green glowing bright and true. 'But most importantly,' he added, needing to lighten up before he said something really stupid, 'you love opera and you love Italian food—thus a truly cultured woman.'

'You're so parochial.' She growled, but she was still smiling.

'Look, you even know long words.'

'And patronising.'

'Don't forget debonair.'

'Arrogant.'

'And a good dancer.'

'Did we mention arrogant already?'

'You love me for it.'

'If I were to love you, it would be in spite of it.'

He chuckled and spun her away from him before pulling her tight again. 'I haven't had this much fun in ages.'

'You mean this much sex.' Her eyes glinted.

'That's true. And, honestly, I've been on the lookout for a secluded corner but there aren't any. Terrible.' He yanked her even closer and brushed his nose against hers. 'But I'm still having fun.'

Her chin tilted. 'So where did you learn to dance?'

'Boarding school. Ms Brady.' He swept her into another turn, then caught her close again, making her thighs sandwich one of his so their hips and torsos were plastered together.

'She might have taught you the waltz but I don't believe she taught you to bump and grind quite like this.' She was breathless now.

'Oh, no. Ms Brady was quite young. It was her first year of teaching…my last year of school…' He waggled his brows.

'Luca!'

He dropped his arm, dipping her head and shoulders backwards down almost to the floor, leant over her and laughed and laughed. Finally forgetting everything except how good he felt when she was close.

Emily came upright, still laughing, and then utterly relaxed into his deliciously tight embrace. She hadn't danced in—

well, ever. She'd always been working, too tired to go clubbing and she'd never been invited to a ball or anything as elite as this. Now she'd discovered how much fun it was, or how much fun it was when she had Luca to lead her—and Luca like this? With his smooth words and even smoother moves that seemed so real and so nice... Oh, she was utterly sunk now.

Several songs later, she slipped away from him. Needing a break from the way he was teasing her—and he was teasing her again. She could see the spark in his eye, he knew exactly what he was doing to her and how hot she was feeling—hot, and so happy.

In the powder room, a woman who Emily knew was one of the bigwigs of the evening came alongside her.

'It's so lovely you could be here,' she said with a bright smile. 'We weren't expecting Luca to come tonight, let alone bring a date.'

Emily simply smiled back, not sure how she should handle this. Luca hadn't exactly introduced her as his date, but then he had just been dirty dancing with her in front of everyone.

'He's a very generous donor,' the woman added.

'Of course.' Emily nodded. He would support cancer research—she could still hear that rough loathing in his voice when he'd told her about his mother dying.

'She was so young.'

Emily nodded again. She must have been as her son was only seven when she died.

'And they'd only just married.' The woman uncapped her lipstick. 'So tragic.'

Emily froze. 'Yes,' she murmured. Just married. The woman wasn't talking about Luca's mother at all. She was talking about his *wife*.

She went back out to the ballroom. He had taken a seat near some other guests but slightly removed—an empty chair between him and the others. That was him, wasn't it? Isolated. He looked up and saw her, a heart-melting smile flashed and he pulled that empty chair a little closer to him. Feeling like a fraud, she sat in it.

'You OK?' he asked quietly in her ear. 'You look a bit pale.'

'Just a bit tired.' She listened to the music and all the while longed to let the pleasure mount as Luca, who had quietly taken possession of her hand, ran his fingers over the links of the bracelet and over her wrist. But she couldn't relax again. She twisted her fingers, to link them through his. He let her, but she knew there was a vast crevasse between them—one she had to try to bridge. 'What was her name?'

He turned a questioning gaze on her.

'Your wife,' she blurted before caution could stop her.

For a moment he looked utterly shocked. Then everything shuttered. And she had to grip his fingers to stop them slipping away from hers.

'What happened to her?' She longed to know. 'What was she like?'

He jerked his hand away then. 'I don't want to talk about it.'

She saw guilt wash over his face just before he clamped down on it and froze over.

* * *

Luca stood, his blood running through him cold enough to make him shiver. 'Do you mind if we go now?'

She said nothing, just rose next to him and pulled the wrap closer about her shoulders. He didn't take her arm, just walked alongside her to the exit. He didn't phone Ricardo, it was faster to get a cab and he needed to move quickly.

He sat on the edge of the seat, staring at the window as they were driven. All he could see was the needle to administer the pain relief, he could smell the antiseptic and he could hear the beep of the machine as every few minutes the medicine was added, drop by drop, trying to keep her comfortable as life ebbed.

But he couldn't see her face. He'd forgotten. *What was she like?* In the second that Emily had asked he couldn't have answered.

'Her name was Nikki.' Reminding himself more than telling her. 'We met at Oxford. Some party or other. She was fluent in French and German. I spoke Italian and Spanish. We joked we'd take over the continent.'

He had loved her, hadn't he? He'd thought he had. Had thought he could feel nothing deeper…but that memory was fading now under the glare of this present madness and he hated that. He felt fickle and disloyal and he wanted to reject the thing that was doing this to him.

'She had brown eyes, dark hair. Tall, slim. French as anything.' He fought to capture her image. 'She was headstrong, a little spoilt. A lot spoilt actually. She could be moody but some of that was…' The memories were all back now. 'She could have gone out with anyone but she went with me.' Vivacious, petulant, young and, all of a sudden, gone.

Afterwards he'd filled his life with work and the drive to succeed—and he had, financially at least. And he'd succeeded in sealing himself away. Not running the risk of loss again, keeping his heart within his control—not wanting or needing anyone else. Because he hadn't had anyone to embrace him, not since he was little—a time he could hardly remember. And when he'd grown up, the one time he'd found someone she'd been taken from him.

'It was so fast. She was always slim but all of a sudden she was skeletal. And before we even knew about it there was nothing they could do to stop it.'

A hand touched his—soft. An even softer voice spoke. 'I'm sorry you lost her, Luca.'

He closed his eyes, clamped down on his jaw. Hating himself all the more because his first thought in response to that statement was just not right. How could he have let a few hot moments wipe all that history out? What kind of man was he?

This lust threatened him, sparked uncontrolled, frankly wrong emotions. He inhaled, fighting the nausea that rose at the mishmash of images in his head. He needed to step back—abstain rather than indulge.

'I'm really tired,' he said lamely as they entered his house. 'I'm just going to go straight to bed.'

'OK.'

He tuned out the soft acquiescence in her voice. He did not want her understanding or interfering or caring. He did not want *anything* from her—especially not her warm and welcoming comfort. He clenched every muscle, walking faster to the private prison that his room had become.

Emily watched him go and felt her heart tearing more with every step. He looked haunted. She shouldn't have asked. Curiosity wasn't good for cats and it wasn't good for her. She ached all over—wishing she could help him, wishing she could help herself. Why was it that she had fallen for someone who couldn't love her the way she needed? Who didn't want her love?

He might think she was good enough to take on a date, good enough to mix with whomever. But none of that mattered now—because how could she even try to compete with his dead wife?

CHAPTER THIRTEEN

THE day was one of the longest Luca had ever endured. His body ached as if he'd been competing in some high-performance multi-sport event. Ha. Some iron man he was. Abstinence was not the answer. He hadn't slept for a second of the previous night. Lying there battling desire and the demons of the past and an anger that he could scarcely control—at the way Emily had invaded everything. At the way she'd made him think terrible things. When she had said she was sorry he'd lost Nikki, he'd had his worst moment yet—because right then he hadn't been sorry. He'd just wanted to rewind to those moments on the dance floor with Emily—to go back to forgetting and having fun.

He felt terrible for that—was all the more determined to find a way to rip her out of his life. But the hunger, the instinct driving him meant he hunted her out the minute he got home, winding his arms around her, hoping she could fill the void that seemed to be gaping wide within him. He looked into her sea-green eyes, saw the new shadows in them, the way her gaze skittered from his.

'I can't seem to stay away from you for long,' he said.

'And that's a bad thing?'

He heard the hurt and felt even more upset. This wasn't her fault. He was trapped—no matter which way he turned he seemed to be doing things wrong.

'I'm sorry.'

'What for?'

For not being what she needed. For not being the man he thought he was. For having the thoughts he did.

He kissed her, the way she ought to be kissed. And in that kiss he felt himself falling, so close to giving in. It seemed as though every time they'd had sex he was stripped of more of his finesse and now he was overcome with the urge to just hold tight and pump—the most basic instinct. Wanting to take her, to fill her, to claim her absolutely. The temptation was so strong—how could it feel so right when in his head he knew it was wrong?

She sat astride him, her skin pale gold, silky soft, and yet he could feel the strength in her thighs as she rode him. Eye sparkling, face flushed, her breasts swaying to the rhythm she was setting. There was no self-consciousness now, just pure pleasure, sensual delight. Only now he didn't think he was going to be able to keep up with her. Only now did he realise this wasn't how he wanted it to be—this wasn't all he wanted to be. Emotion overwhelmed him.

'I'm going to come.' His voice was hoarse.

'Are you now?' Her eyes flashed. 'I don't think so.'

'I don't think you can stop me,' he gasped. 'I don't think *I* can stop me.'

She knelt up and off him.

Groaning, he shook his head, disbelief flooding him. 'I'm still going to come. Just by *looking* at you.'

He stretched his arms wide, large hands gripping the sheet, trying to stay in control. 'You are magnificent. The most beautiful woman.'

She bent forward, whispered in his ear. 'Don't hold back, Luca. Dive in with me.'

Oh, God, he didn't deserve her, couldn't resist her, gave everything as he gave in. Rolling them both over, he rose high, thrust long and deep and hard and held her tight.

She arched up, her neck bared, her puff of laughter lost in a cry of joyous, erotic freedom. And he was lost—held nothing back, utterly sunk in the blaze of feeling pouring through him.

He'd changed. He was whispering something in his first language. There was almost desperation in his touch. Gone was the languorous lover who skilfully guided them to ecstasy and beyond. Instead his fingers gripped her so hard they pinched and she was sure he wasn't even aware of it as he gathered her even closer and plunged even deeper. His kisses were passionate and landing all over as if he couldn't decide where to go next and was frantically trying to touch her everywhere all at once. And the breathless phrase in Italian was louder now, muttered and repeated and under the onslaught it was easy to remember. Afterwards he held her close, raining gentle kisses that soothed her to slumber while over and over he muttered it.

* * *

She woke much earlier than usual. Her legs were weighted down by something hard and heavy—and alive.
Luca.

Shouldn't he have been long gone by now? Warm excitement rushed through her system—but he hadn't gone, he'd wanted to stay. He was tucked up close behind her, his leg and arm thrown over her. Slowly, carefully, she turned. Not wanting to wake him. Not wanting him to leave just yet. She looked at him as he rested, the dark brows relaxed, his mouth full and soft. His broad shoulder a gleaming golden brown, contrasting against the crisp white of the sheets.

His eyes opened and she stilled utterly—her breathing, even her heart, stopped for a beat. Three beats.

The dark chocolate in his eyes was liquid and warm and he regarded her for a long moment in silence. The hard centre was smaller, but it was still there. She watched, anxious that it might grow and that the glow in his face would dim.

But it was his arm that tightened as he pulled her back against him, pushing her down to the mattress again. 'Sleep.'

When next she woke he was kissing her face, gentle kisses on her brow and cheek and jaw, and his hands were stroking down the sides of her torso.

'Morning breath OK?' he teased.

She smiled and inside the flames in her heart roared. She caught his mouth with hers and as the morning sun warmed the bed her confidence surged.

'What does it mean?' she asked.

'What does what mean?'

'*Siete il fuoco della mia anima.*' Nerves suddenly hit as she felt him tense. 'It's what you said to me last night.'

'Oh.' All frozen now. 'It's nothing.' Reluctance written all over him.

She waited.

'It's just a turn of phrase. An expression.' He might still be in her bed but he'd withdrawn so far he might as well be on the moon.

She waited some more but there was nothing else. And her sense of delight burst with a bang. All the good vibes gushed out, leaving her flat and angry.

'Oh, I get it. Nothing special, right?' She sat up, clutching the sheet to her chest. Too hurt to stop herself attacking. 'It's what you say to whoever you're sleeping with. That way it doesn't matter if you forget my name. That sum it up right, Luca?'

'You know there is no one else in my life. You *know*.'

Not right now. Not living.

And what she didn't know was why he was suddenly going cold again when last night had been so incredibly magical.

'Don't complicate this.' He sat up too, pushing the sheet away.

'Don't deny this already is complicated.' This was a mess.

He swung his legs out of the bed. Well, his 'end of conversation' attitude wasn't going to wash with her. And with a reckless courage she didn't know she had, she brought the issue right out into the open.

'Do you feel anything for me, Luca?'

He turned a burning hard gaze on her, clearly angry with the question. 'You know how much I want you.'

Sex. He always brought it back to sex. The lowest common denominator, but surely he recognised how much more there was to bind them? How was it that he could have given so much to her physically—given himself up in her arms—and yet try to remain so withdrawn emotionally? How could he divorce the two so completely? She didn't believe he could and she hated his denial.

She saw his anger rising, but she'd never been angrier herself. He was incredibly strong, incredibly determined. She had one hell of a battle on her hands and she couldn't help the feeling that she'd picked the losing side.

'Get out, Luca, since you so obviously regret being in here.'

He walked. She slumped down in the bed and stared hard and long at the ceiling. Determined not to cry. Determined to get on with her life. Knowing she needed an action plan much sooner than later.

When Luca came up from the most unsatisfying swim of his life he found her on the floor of the lounge surrounded by pamphlets and forms. 'What are you doing?'

'Figuring out my future.'

'Oh.' Every muscle inside got a shot of adrenalin. 'What are you going to do?'

'I'm going to teach music.'

He glanced at the pamphlets. Some were for university courses, some for a college of music—in *Ireland*? Hell, there were some travel ones in there? He grappled with the

iolent urge to grab them and toss them in the bin and keep
er hostage like some fifth-century warlord. The urge itself
nade him even madder—shouldn't he be feeling relieved?
Those who can, do. Those who can't, teach.'

'How insulting.' She stood and stomped towards the
kitchen. 'Teachers aren't made, they're born.' She whirled
back to face him. 'There are a few things I could teach
ou.'

'OK. That was rude of me.' But the frustration was real.
Why, when for the first time in your life you're free to do
anything you want? Do you want to take a job where it's
all about other people?'

'Why do you encourage me to do whatever I want and
then knock down the one thing I do want to do? Why can't
you understand that I like working with people?'

'But you have so much talent. So much potential—you
could do anything.' She could. He wanted to see her seize
the opportunity—wanted her to fly.

'I *like* teaching, Luca. I'm sorry if it's not glamorous or
good enough for you.'

He drew a breath. Saw he'd really offended her when
all he wanted was for her to reach for what she truly
wanted. 'Of course it's good enough—'

'I don't need high-powered kudos to prove my worth the
way you do.' She was on the attack now.

'What does that mean?'

'Well, come on, Luca,' she sneered. 'How many hours
do you have to work? How many quadrillions do you
have to make? Who is it you're trying so damn hard to impress, huh?'

'No one,' he choked.

Yeah, right—she didn't even have to say it aloud.

'I work the hours I do because I like the challenge of i I like to be the best.' Proving a point? Perhaps it had starte that way—to be more of a success than his father had beer and utterly without his help or interest. Now it was mor of a habit than anything.

'But what about other things, Luca?'

'Like what? I have a great life.'

'You have a half-life. You work so you can escape th things everyone else wants to embrace.'

'Like what?'

'Love.' She threw the word at him.

The silence was sudden and total. He couldn't hav moved if he'd tried.

She turned away with a sigh. 'Luca, you've been so gen erous. I'd been caring for Kate and worrying about finding money for bread for so damn long that I didn't have time to even dream my own dreams. You've given me that time.

'And teaching really is your dream?'

'Yes. Simple as it may seem to you, it's what I want to do. It's what I'm happy doing.'

Well, OK, then. 'How can I—?'

Her phone buzzed.

'—help.' But she'd answered. Her sister. He could hear her tones even from this distance—asking for a favour. He listened to Emily's replies, her 'yes' and 'sure' and 'no problem, I'll be there' and grew edgy again.

He waited 'til she ended the call. 'Why do you let her take advantage of your generous nature?'

* * *

'She's not…' Emily paused. He didn't get it, did he? She liked to help those she loved—that wasn't being taken advantage of by them, that was doing things because she cared. So she threw sarcasm back at him—proving her own painful point. 'But isn't that what you're doing, Luca? Taking advantage of my generous nature?'

Taking advantage of the fact that she'd fallen for him and could deny him nothing?

Solemn, he met her challenge. 'What if I am? You should cut your losses and run.'

'Maybe I will,' she answered honestly. 'But right now there's this.'

She walked towards him, bolder than ever, kissed him hard. There was no mercy left in the desire that raged between them. But she pushed back before it got too far. 'It's still there. As strong as ever.'

His nod was almost imperceptible but it was enough to give her the shot of courage she needed. She stepped close again, asked very softly, 'Would my loving you be so bad?'

He stood stock-still. Then she saw the flexing muscle in his jaw, the impossible fight to stop colour tainting his cheeks. Then his eyes narrowed and she braced, sensing that he was not going to be nice.

'You're always helping people. *Caring* for people. Where's your selfishness?'

'Everything I do stems from selfishness, Luca. I like to be needed. I have to be needed. If there's no one who wants or needs me, then what do I have?'

'Freedom.'

She shook her head. 'That's not the kind of freedom I

want. I need a community, a family, a place to fit—to be necessary to. Otherwise I'm aimless and lonely. And there's no one for me. I do things for people and hope that one day I'll be given to and cared for too.'

That he would give back to her—just what he could. She'd be happy with that, wouldn't she? But his expression was rock-hard and she tried to hide the fact that he was breaking her heart. She railed against his silence—his denial—wanting to scream with frustration and futility.

'No man is an island, Luca. Not even you.' She began to fail at hiding her frustration. 'You help people too. You try to maintain this distance and you can't.'

His gaze dropped.

'I know what you've done for Micaela and Ricardo. Their family.'

He looked back then, surprised. 'How do you know that?'

'She told me.'

'That's nothing. That's just money.'

'I know about the toy cupboard you keep for Marco. He showed me.'

'Again. Money.'

'Rubbish. That's caring. You *like* these people, Luca. You care about them and you do things for them.'

'It's entirely self-serving. Better to have Marco's little hands occupied with some trains than scribbling on my walls.'

She gave him a yeah-right look. 'Try as you might to deny it, you're involved in these people's lives. Their hapiness matters to you. You care about them.' *And you care about me too.*

Their eyes met. She wondered if he'd caught her telepathic add-on.

'You take risks with money. You take huge risks. High risk, high return, right? Ever thought it might be the same with your heart?' She had gone so far, there was no point in holding back. 'And the thing is, Luca, I'm a safe bet.'

'I have to…' He trailed off. 'Go to work. I've really got to go to work.'

For the second time that day she watched him walk away from her. His usually graceful body looked awkward, as if he was having to concentrate hard on every small movement. She wrapped her arms around herself and hugged. Oh, hell, was she deluding herself completely?

OK. So he was still in love with his wife. That didn't mean he couldn't still care about her. This could work. She could settle for that, couldn't she? But suddenly she felt vulnerable and lost. Bitterness surged. Why should she be the one to do the loving all the time? Why couldn't she have someone to love her back completely?

She did, she realised now, want it all. And he wasn't capable of giving it.

He'd got as far as the door when all her selfishness burst out. 'You know I've tried it your way but this whole hedonistic holiday thing just isn't me.' She took a deep breath. 'I need more. I want more. From you.'

He froze, back to her, hand on the door. 'You said you just wanted sex too.'

'I did. I do. But I've changed my mind.' She flung her head up. 'Woman's prerogative.'

His head was bowed. 'Emily, I...'

Hope crashed down as she heard the crack in his voice. 'It's OK. I know already. You don't have to explain.'

He'd buried his heart. He didn't want to try again. His hand tightened on the door. Finally he jerked it open and was gone.

CHAPTER FOURTEEN

Luca had been trying to catch his breath for hours, his heart thumping one uneven beat ahead of the rest of him. He couldn't sit still, couldn't settle, couldn't concentrate. All he could see was Emily asking him, *Would my loving you be so bad?*

He shut down the computer and flicked off the monitor. There was no point pretending any more. His work day was over before it had even begun.

Siete il fuoco della mia anima—he hadn't realised he'd been saying it aloud. And when she'd said it back to him it had freaked him out—he hadn't wanted to admit it to himself, let alone her. But it was true. *Sua anima…suo cuove.*

The sheer velocity of it stunned him. She was like a meteorite, hurtling into his world, causing chaos and upheaval. The ground was shifting beneath his feet and he was *quaking*. He needed to talk to her, to tell her, to ask her for patience. He knew he'd get it. She was loving and strong but he couldn't quite believe in it yet. He wondered if she was still even there.

He ran. All the way home he ran, not caring about the

strange looks people gave him as he sprinted the mile or so in his three-piece suit.

She was lying on the sofa, reading, looking a little pale and turning even more so as she watched him come near. Did she regret their earlier conversation? He wanted to close his eyes against the depths he saw in hers. The courage.

'Are you OK?' She really did look pale.

She nodded. Emotion rushed through him. Yes, he wanted her to love him. He wanted, he wanted, he wanted—absolutely everything she had to offer he would take. But he didn't think he could do that any more without risk to himself. It meant opening doors he'd tried to seal shut long ago and he didn't know if he had the strength to let her open them.

Who was he kidding? She'd already streaked through them and was firmly lodged in place, wasn't she? Right in his heart. That didn't mean he was happy about it.

'I need some time, Emily.'

'Time for what?'

'To adjust to this. To us.' There had been nothing slow about their affair—and that was as much his fault as hers. He pushed physically, she pushed emotionally. Together that made for one hell of a ride.

And what would she say once she knew it all? If he told her what was really in his heart, would she really still be there for him? He couldn't trust that she would. So it wasn't talking that he'd do yet. He'd love her first, and hold his breath as he told her after.

She winced as she sat up.

'You sure you're OK?' he asked, sitting down beside her.

'Just a tummy ache. I'm fine.'

Anxiety perhaps? He stroked the back of his fingers down the side of her face, wanted to reassure them both with his touch, willing her to understand.

Her expression softened. He couldn't have said a thing then anyway. He opened his arms and she leant into them. He kissed her hair, her cheek, her mouth, pulled her closer.

Another wince.

Concerned, he leaned back to look into her face. 'You're not up to it?'

'No, I want to,' she murmured. 'But...' She was blushing.

He paused. He was so hard, it cost a lot to slow down—she caused irreparable damage to his heart.

'It's just that I'm bleeding a little.'

'Bleeding?'

'Just, you know, a little. It's nothing.'

No, he didn't know. 'But you said you had your period a couple of weeks ago.' Confusion. Fast followed by fear. 'You shouldn't be bleeding now.'

She sat up, wincing again, and then stood, pulling her tee shirt down as she walked away from him. 'I'm a bit out of sorts. I'm fine.'

Out of sorts? Abnormal bleeding was a little more than out of sorts. She wasn't telling him all of it. He could see it in the stiffness of her back. His alarm bells rang louder. What were her other symptoms? How long had she been feeling like this? 'Have you got a headache?'

'If I didn't before I do now.'

He ignored the irony. She was getting more angry, more defensive. So there must be more to it. 'I think you should see a doctor.'

'Luca. I'm fine.'

But anxiety had a hold of him now and thoughts and nightmare visions swirled before him. He went rigid—trying to reject this reality and control the queasiness clogging his ability to process. He stood, headed straight to the phone on the bench. Not again. He was not going through this again.

'You're seeing a doctor. I'll call him right away.' He'd get an immediate appointment. Insist on it. Pay whatever. House call if necessary. He wanted to know what it was and how it could be fixed. *Now*.

Emily stared at the implacable determination driving Luca and exasperation made her raise her voice and overcome her embarrassment. 'Put the phone down, Luca. I'm ovulating, all right?'

That stopped him. 'What?'

'Ovulating. I get a spot of bleeding and tenderness in the tummy. It's called mittelschmerz. It's perfectly normal and lots of women get it.'

'Ovulating?' Clearly dazed, he tried to put the phone back on its base but it missed with a clatter.

'Ovulating.' She nodded.

'Ovulating.' Still confused.

'Happens every month.' She nodded more, exaggerated fashion.

'Ov—'

'Yes, Luca.' Her patience vaporised. '*Ovulating*. You know, where my ovary releases an egg and it goes down the… Do you really need all the details?'

He drew an audible breath and shook his head and she watched as his gaze travelled to her breasts, to her belly. He looked totally blown away. 'Ov… OK… Well… You take a lie-down or something.'

'Right.' She went to her room to escape him as much as anything. She still wanted him, yearned for him. Her body was burning, screaming at her to mate and make love and life with him—literally in heat.

Instead she curled into a ball and wondered how long she was going to have to wait.

She must have fallen asleep because the sun was late-afternoon high in the sky when she came to.

He was standing near the lounge window looking out, but as she walked towards him she could tell that he wasn't seeing any of the spectacular view across the park. His eyes were unfocused, and whatever it was he was seeing, it was causing him pain. His mouth was set, the corners tilting down. Jaw locked. His arms barred across his chest and she could see his hands curled into fists. Fighting.

He turned. His stance didn't relax. If anything he went even more rigid. She forced herself to take another step forward, bracing against the chill sweeping from him to her. His jaw was still locked. She saw the muscle flick as he clenched harder on his teeth.

Her own jaw tensed in response and she had to concentrate hard to be able to move it and use her voice. 'Luca?'

'Emily.' His voice was flat. He seemed to be deciding how to say whatever it was he was going to say. 'I…'

And suddenly, blindingly, she knew. She knew what it

was. And then pride got in there and made her take over. 'You don't want me to stay here any more, do you?'

His eyes met hers. Unwavering. 'No.'

For a second, or maybe longer, she was struck still. Listening, hearing that vehement admission echo louder and louder in her head.

Well, she had asked for it, hadn't she—that he never lie to her? But it was such a shock—that he could go from that adoring lover who'd cradled her to sleep last night to…

That all-preserving pride reared up again. She whirled on the spot.

'You don't have to go right away.'

'No, Luca,' she corrected. 'I do.' As if she were going to hang around for another night after this? What the hell did he expect? Farewell sex?

'Where will you go?'

She paused. Kate didn't need her any more. Luca didn't want her. 'I might try somewhere new.'

She turned her head then, wanting a glimpse of him at this moment—masochist that she was.

His face was pale but set. She knew that determination. He wasn't going to change his mind and she refused to humiliate herself by trying to make him. She'd been trying to do that for too long.

Idly she wondered what her own face was like—because right now, for this second, she felt nothing. Then a touch of irritation flared at the way he was just standing there, staring back at her. If it was over, it was over. He didn't need to watch for the meltdown. She refused to give him the meltdown. God, she'd given him everything else. Dignity was the one thing she had left to hold onto.

'Will you give me a minute? I'd like to get my things together.'

His head jerked. 'I'll go for a walk. Be an hour or so. Then I can drop you wherever you want.'

Stiffly he walked from the room. She stared at the door he'd closed behind him. Seeing through it, at the way he just kept on walking. Just like that.

Had he forgotten he held her heart in his hands? Because he'd just clenched his fists and now her heart was squashed and bleeding and hurting all the more because he'd done it. He'd hurt her and he'd known he would and he hadn't stopped.

Starkly he'd revealed the disparity in their feelings towards each other. Because if he felt for her at all—even as a friend—he wouldn't have done this so cruelly. So coldly ruthless.

She went to the window he'd been frowning out of, looked down to the footpath in front of the building. A second later he appeared. A stupid last curl of hope unfurled. If he looked back up to her…if he looked back up…

But he walked away, no backwards glance, no apparent care in the world.

CHAPTER FIFTEEN

IT WAS warm that late summer evening but Luca felt as if nothing could heat him up—not even the flames of hell. That was where he was now. Locked in a nightmare world of past and present.

His mother had gradually faded away, as if the frustration inside was eating her. The cancer growing and spreading slowly like the poison it was. Nikki's was fast—so fast and there had been nothing they could do to fight it. Memories swirled. He hated them.

To watch someone he loved suffer. To have someone he loved be taken from him wasn't something he could go through again. When she'd winced this afternoon and told him of her tummy ache he'd been consumed by nightmares and demons. Dread fear that she too was going to slip away from him. The fright he'd got was enough to shatter the fragile vision he'd been building—of being with her.

Only then she'd told him. It wasn't a sickness—an unknown cancer killing her. Instead it was her body signalling that it was ready to create life.

A mixture of terror and longing washed through him.

He was never going to marry again, certainly never going to have children. Never going to set himself up for rejection and pain and unstoppable loss. He'd been through enough of that and he'd chosen to live a life that would be satisfied by the challenges of his career. He'd had to pull away from her.

But now, confronted with the prospect of returning to that life, he knew he didn't want to. It was empty, unfulfilling and all the money in the world couldn't buy him what he really wanted. *High risk, high return.* She'd said she was a safe bet...but she wasn't. No one was. There were no answers to the questions that had him trapped.

She couldn't promise not to die, not to leave him.

He walked through the gardens, not seeing the trees or lawn as he grappled with the problem. Desperately searching for the answer he needed because inexorably he was being drawn back to her. He wanted her—he loved her—he had to face it: for as long as she wanted him, he was hers.

And there it was, his answer. If she could promise that she wouldn't leave him for as long as she lived, then he could take it on. Because he would promise the same; he could say nothing truer.

She had been so dignified. So understanding. It hurt him more than if she'd cried. And it angered him too. Why hadn't she fought for him? Why hadn't she yelled at him? He'd wanted her to yell at him, to declare everything again. He'd wanted to hear it from her one more time.

God, he really was selfish.

Why should she? He suddenly saw the unreasonable demands he'd put on her—asking for everything when what had he offered in return? Nothing. Nothing but denial, denial, denial of how much she meant to him. Of what she meant to him.

He couldn't let her go without explaining everything. Whether she would still want to stay after that, he didn't know. Guilt washed through him once more. How he felt just wasn't right. But it was how it was, and he needed to tell her. He could only hope her heart was big enough to still love him once she knew. It was the one thing that brought him a sliver of warmth back.

Emily was just keeping back the tears as she packed. She started by folding her clothing neatly, but a couple of items into it she was frenzied, tossing them into her open bag. She had to get out of there. Hurry before she lost it.

But even as she forced herself to speed up the first tear trickled. Acidic. She was hot all over and her heart was thumping and up in her throat for her to gag on.

'Damn.' She swore, sniffed, stuffed the tee shirt in with the others and wiped her cheek with the back of her hand. Another burning tear streaked down.

Hands gripped her shoulders and pulled her back against a strong, hard body. 'Emily.'

She hardly recognised his voice. But she knew the feel of him. And it was that touch that made her lose it completely.

'No,' she shouted as she turned in his arms. She would not let him try to comfort her. Not now. 'Don't do this to me. Don't DO this!' she screamed at him, pushing him away with every ounce of her strength.

But her strength was nothing on his and his embrace only tightened. 'Stop crying, Emily. Please stop crying.'

'Don't be so cruel, Luca.' She hardly heard the break in his voice through her own sobs of anguish. 'I can't touch you again. I don't want you to touch me again. I can't live through this if you do, Luca. So don't.'

He dropped his arms. His face was white. 'I'm sorry. I—'

'Don't tell me you're sorry!' She smeared tears across her face and sniffed. 'Don't pity me or patronise me!'

'Emily—'

'Just leave me alone!' she yelled at him. 'Why can't you leave me just a shred of dignity? Leave me alone so I can go.' The humiliation was total.

'I don't want you to go.'

She stared at him, almost crumpling under the pain and confusion.

He stared back, stock-still, pale, as low-voiced he repeated it. 'I don't want you to go, Emily.'

Fresh tears filled her eyes and flooded over their rims.

'I know I've hurt you. It was the last thing I wanted to do.'

But she'd always known he would, hadn't she? And so had he. That was why he'd frowned at the beginning. Why he'd tried to impose rules. Why he'd said it so many times—I don't want to hurt you—because he'd known he would. It was why she'd felt that nagging warning. But it was impossible. Feelings, emotions, love seeped between the lines and through the cracks. Mercurial. It couldn't be stopped—well, hers couldn't anyway. He on the other hand? He was the impenetrable fortress. The one who'd locked his heart away for ever and fair enough.

So now she refused to listen. She loved him. He couldn't love her. That was all she needed to know. There was nothing more to it.

'I can't stay here any more, Luca. I can't do this any more.'

The last half hour had been the most hellishly painful of her life and she couldn't cope with it being drawn out another day or two, week or two. It had to be over. Her father had not cared enough to live for her. Kate no longer needed her. And Luca—the man she'd fallen so utterly in love with—didn't want her. And the pain of his rejection was so intense she could hardly breathe, could hardly walk, could hardly bear to stay conscious.

So she fought it, storming past, not wanting him to witness her weakness. Wanting privacy for just a moment of self-indulgence when she could scream and cry before pulling herself back together and getting on with it like the good old trouper she was.

She made straight for the door, heedless of her bare feet. She just had to get out of there *now* because she really was going to howl.

She got as far as the hall when his hand grasped her upper arm and pulled. His other arm came around her waist. By this stage her tears were blinding and she couldn't see where he was half lifting, half dragging her.

A door slammed and his hands left her and she stumbled forward a few more paces.

'Damn it, Luca, what more do you want from me?' She'd offered him everything she had and he'd refused it, yet still he demanded.

She turned to face him. He had his back to the door. Looming big, still pale and more serious than she'd ever seen him.

'Where…?' She trailed off. She knew already.

'My room.' Relentlessly he stared at her. *'Mine.'*

Every cell quivered at the force in his reply. Racked by another sob, she quickly moved, determined to stuff all her emotion back in. Turning her back to him, she blinked and tried to focus on the furnishings, the floor—anything but the misery she'd seen reflected in his eyes. There was no glimmer of hope or happiness there and she didn't want to prolong the agony a minute more than necessary.

There wasn't a thing out of place. The doors to the walk-in wardrobe were open and she could see his suits hanging neatly. There were still no personal touches. No family photos. Only a stack of books and magazines by one side of the bed to indicate some sort of personality inhabited the room. But it wasn't sterile. It was a calm, quiet, restful space. Her shaking inside only increased and she gripped every muscle even harder, trying to piece herself back together and keep it that way. She heard him exhale, a harsh long breath.

'Please let me explain. Please, Emily.'

When had she ever been able to say no to him?

'I need to talk to you about Nikki.'

No. She ached to scream it. Jerked as if to stop herself. Put her hand on her ribcage—trying to protect herself from more pain striking deep. She didn't think she could listen to him and survive.

'Please, Emily. It won't take long.'

He was blocking the door. She had no escape. Head

bowed, fists clenched against her chest, she kept her back to him as she summoned that last grain of courage. She heard every word.

'You know we met at Oxford. She was eighteen, I was almost twenty. I was her first boyfriend and she was the first woman I'd dated for more than a couple of weeks. One day she woke with a bad head. She thought it was monthly. She used to get migraines a bit...' His voice faded. 'I never knew it could be so fast. She had no chance—no time to even *try* to fight it.'

Emily's heart was aching in a different way now. Not just for herself, but for him and for Nikki. She turned and looked at him. He was still focused on her, still relentless, as if he had decided on a path and was determined to take it—no matter what the cost. And there was a cost—she could see it as his eyes grew darker, dominating his whitened face, and she could hear it in his thinning, rasping tone.

'She wanted to get married. It was her wish—one of life's great milestones to achieve before...' He cleared his throat, fought to put strength back into his voice. 'She was going to miss out on everything else. She wanted one moment of happiness. And it was one thing I *could* do for her...' He faded out again. 'She died nine hours later.'

Emily just stared at him. Unable to see anything but the scene he'd painted for her and the unspeakable sadness of that day.

'Don't cry.'

She didn't realise she still was. She wiped away the wet from her cheeks. 'You've never gotten over her.'

'No.' The wince of pain that screwed up his face for a second was as if she'd struck him a mortal blow. 'But not in the way you mean.' His agony seemed to throb in the air. 'It was awful, Emily. And after seeing Mum fade away, and then Nikki be torn down by that hideous disease, I decided no, I'm not going to be in that position again. I put all my energy into my business. I didn't want intimacy. I've never had a relationship since, never spent the whole night with a woman, never had a woman stay in my apartment even. Occasional, casual flings. One-night stands. And then for a long time nothing. Too busy with work.' Flat now, he explained, 'I didn't want a woman—or anyone—to become a necessary part of my life. I didn't want a relationship to form. I didn't want to be hurt when it ended. So I always ended it before it had the chance to begin.'

His hedonistic, no-strings approach hadn't been care-free, it had been underpinned by loss and heartbreak and denial.

'You must have really loved her.'

Her comment seemed to etch greater pain into his face, lines of agony carved deep with a knife and bleeding. 'I used to think I did.' His knuckles were white. 'But do you want to know the awful truth, Emily? Do you want to know what I really feel?'

Silently she waited, because the despair in him was close to the surface now and she wanted to know what it was, why it was.

'*Glad.*' He ground the admission out on a wave of self-disgust. 'Part of me feels glad it happened—that she's gone.' His breathing had gone harsh, his chest jerking. 'Because I. Want. You.'

He looked appalled even as he said it. 'I look back now and wonder if I ever loved her, when how I feel about you is so intense—so all-consuming. So absolutely terrifying. And if I thought losing Nikki was bad, it's nothing on how it would be to lose you.' His voice rose higher and the words came faster. 'It's not that I don't want you. It's that I don't *want* to want you. Not like this. Not when it makes me question everything, not when it makes me feel *relieved* that I'm free to chase you. How awful does that make me? What kind of a man am I?'

He suddenly stopped. Suddenly looked utterly vulnerable, utterly afraid. 'Can you really love a man who thinks like that?'

'Luca, stop.' She took the few paces over to him, grasped his fist in her hands. 'Stop torturing yourself.'

But his heart was rent open and she saw the depth of it—the pain he'd suffered, the loneliness he'd made himself endure and the strength he'd used to seal it all away.

'You did love her. Of course you did. You married her. You gave her what she wanted. You put her first. That is love.' She spoke gently but firmly. 'And you've become the man you are, capable of feeling the depth of feeling that you can, because of her. She taught you love and sacrifice and loss. You did love her.'

'But not like this.' He shook his head.

Emily squeezed her fingers over his. 'It's different. Of course it is. I'm a different person and you're a different person from the one you were back then. It doesn't make the feelings you had for her any less. It's still love. And love isn't measurable, Luca. It isn't comparable. It's just love. And the fear you have of losing me only feels so bad because you've lost before. Not because I'm any more valuable.'

He closed his eyes but she kept talking.

'If she had lived, you would have been happy. We would never have met. We might have passed in the street and you wouldn't have even given me a second glance.'

His smile was faint, as was the slight shake of his head.

Her eyes filled again with the feeling of everything he'd said and hadn't said. 'It's OK to love her, Luca. And it's OK to love me too. It's possible to love more than once, you know.' She took a shaky breath, so badly wanting him to accept her words. 'And you deserve to have been loved by both her *and* me.'

He dropped his face then, hiding the way he was crumbling. And her heart bled for the boy whose mother had gone and whose father had abandoned him and for the youth who had lost his first love so quickly and so cruelly.

She slipped her arms around him and whispered, 'There's a lot to love in you, Luca—there's everything to love.'

His arms snaked around her, pulling her tight as he pressed his face to her neck, and for a long moment he was silent.

'And that's your gift,' he finally mumbled. 'You're so supportive—you have the power to make people feel better.'

'I don't really have a gift, Luca. All I have is love.' And she wanted to give it to him.

His hands tightened. 'That's the greatest gift of all.' He lifted his head and looked at her. 'I don't deserve it for the way I hurt you. But please give it back to me.'

'You already have it. Once it's given, you can't take it back.'

'I know. And now I can't let you go.' He wasn't smiling as he said it. It still troubled him and she knew that if he could, he would let her go. He still felt the fear.

'Do you have a photo of her?' Somehow she had to find peace for them.

He hesitated.

'Show me.'

He stood, and opened the door behind him. She followed him into the next room, eyes widening at the table and bookcases, filing cabinets and high-tech hardware. Some people had a home away from home. It seemed Luca had an office away from the office. He went to the filing cabinet. Opened it and flicked through the obscenely neat files. Her heart splintered more as she saw the way he'd literally tried to put his past in its place and forget about it.

He avoided her eyes as he handed her the picture. It was just a snap. No frame, no album.

Emily looked at the pretty girl, and took in a sharp breath. More tears rolled down her cheeks. She had seen that face before.

'She's Pascal's daughter,' Luca explained, understanding what had made Emily go so still. 'The resemblance is quite something, isn't it?'

Pity swept over Emily. 'Oh, Luca, I'm so sorry.' She felt

terrible. 'And I made you have that dinner with me there. No wonder you were feeling so awkward.'

'And I wanted you to wear something decent—something that would cover you from head to foot and you wore that dress and were so damn irresistible.' He almost smiled. 'Pascal has been unsubtly nagging me to move on for years now. Keeps going on about how wonderful it is to have children.'

'Does he have others?'

'No. It was years of trying before they had her. They would have liked more but it didn't happen for them.'

'Oh, Luca.' Now she saw why Luca had been so determined to help Micaela and Ricardo—wanting them to have it all when his friend had missed out, when he had missed out.

'I guess we're close. We'll always be close.' He looked uncertainly at her, as if asking if that was OK.

'Of course you will.' They had Nikki linking them. Now his parting words to her at the dinner made sense—*he's been cold for too long*. Pascal didn't want that for his son-in-law, he'd been the mentor and guide that Luca had missed out on with his own father and he wanted to see him achieve happiness, not just in his career, but in his personal life too.

'He asked after you last time he emailed.' Luca smiled wryly. 'I think he liked you.'

'I liked him too.' Emily looked at the photo in her hand and then back at Luca. 'Don't confuse the feelings of the past with the feelings of the present. You're a different person now, Luca. She deserves that place in your heart and she would want you to be happy.' She propped the picture up against the lamp on the table. He should have it displayed, just as he should have one of his mum. She'd have a picture of her parents too. She'd see to all that soon. 'She helped make you who you are. And I love the man you are.' She turned to him. 'So strong, Luca.'

'I'm not strong. I've been such a coward and I hurt you. The look on your face…' He paused. 'You deserve better than that. And I'll spend the rest of my life making it up to you.' He glanced over her shoulder to the picture on the desk, seemed to know what Emily was planning, and looked back at her with a new gentleness. 'Thank you for being so generous.'

She shook her head. 'I can afford to be. I have life. I have you.'

His arms swooped around her then and he sighed, pulling her close. 'You gave me such a fright, Emily. I thought you might be sick. I thought I couldn't handle that—but I have no choice.'

And she had one last point to impress on him. 'I've seen what happens when someone gives up, Luca. I've seen someone decide not to bother any more and wither away and die and ignore those who care.' She would be livid if he did that. 'Nikki and your mother would be so angry with you for not living a whole life. Don't use them as your excuse any more. Live now. Live with me. And, heaven forbid, if I do die before you then you just have to pick yourself up and keep on going. Keep on loving.'

But it was her he picked up now, carrying her back through to his bedroom. He laid her down on the bed, looked at her for a long moment before running his hand over her breasts and letting it come to rest low on her belly.

The chocolate in his eyes all sweet fire. 'If we made love now, there's a chance you'd get pregnant?'

'There's every chance, I guess.'

'Is that a risk you're prepared to take with me?'

She'd already gambled her heart on him, so far her reward was priceless and she was starting to hope it was about to multiply many times over. 'High risk, high return, right?'

'*Sì.*' He bent over her, fixing her in place with that burning gaze. 'I've been so wrong. I want to love you. I do love you. So much.'

She melted into the demand of his kiss, softened as he moved his weight onto her. It was a different need he was asking her to fill, no less desperate or passionate, but deeper somehow—total.

'Don't leave me, Emily. Don't ever leave me.' A breathless plea.

She pressed her hand to his heart, feeling the strong beat as she had that first day. 'I'm here, Luca. I'll always be right here.'

There was a brilliance in his face now. '*Siete il fuoco della mia anima*—you are the fire of my soul.' Quietly, deliberately, he translated. '*Mio cuove*—my heart. I mean it. I mean it with all of me—you make me, you are all of me and when I am with you, I know I am alive.'

She cried then, tears of a different kind, tears for herself—of sad relief and sweet disbelief. For the pain and the long years of loneliness and work and heartache— years that she would never regret or resent but was so glad had passed. And he cradled her, comforted her, caressed her. She knew she would never be alone again because her heart was in the care of the strongest, bravest man who was capable of such love. And he showed it to her, kissing away the streams from her eyes, drawing her close, filling her with his strength and holding nothing back. She clung to him, soft and needing every ounce of the sureness of his possession and his passion.

She shuddered in ecstasy as everything he had to offer was given to her, nothing between them now but the powerful surge of love. Every inch of her skin, every muscle, sinew and cell felt it and exulted in it. While she'd had physical completion before, now he gave her emotional fulfilment—telling her with words, eyes and actions how much he loved her. How much he wanted her, needed her and would care for her.

Curled together after, legs and arms and everything between entwined, the warmth having banished the cold and the tears for good, he spoke.

'You haven't said anything about my painting.' He inclined his head and she looked over his shoulder in the direction he'd nodded in.

She hadn't even seen it despite it hanging in perfect position to be viewed from his bed. But now she stared at it. The scene was so familiar. The trees, the topiary… She could almost hear the faint trickle of water from the fountains…could feel the dampness of the air near the grotto…

'I found it in a gallery a few days later and bought it on the spot.'

She studied the richness of it, the graduated greens, the depth and she sank into the memories it invoked: Giardino

Giusti and the most blissful afternoon of her life—sur-
passed by none until now.

She turned back to his steadfast gaze with a dawning
sense of serenity. 'It was the best, wasn't it, Luca?'

'No,' he corrected her with a half-smile, 'it was just the
beginning.'

As her inner peace grew she felt his tension rise again.
She put a hand to his brow, soothing—everything was right
now and he could relax. But his intense look only went
more acute, his molten eyes searching right into her,
suddenly setting *her* soul alight with wonder.

'Do you think you would marry me there, Emily? In the
garden, with a simple ceremony and a picnic under the
trees?'

She blinked but she couldn't stop the burning tingle in
the backs of her eyes, the unstoppable, infinitesimal nod-
ding of her head and the blossoming of absolute joy in her
heart.

'Luca…' the last, the sweetest of her tears spilt, and he
had to draw her shaking body even closer to hear her tiny
whisper '…I think that *that* would be the best.'

And, one fine day, under a blue sky and green branches,
it was.

THE ROYAL HOUSE OF KAREDES

Two crowns, two islands, one legacy

Volume 1 – April 2009
BILLIONAIRE PRINCE, PREGNANT MISTRESS
by Sandra Marton

Volume 2 – May 2009
THE SHEIKH'S VIRGIN STABLE-GIRL
by Sharon Kendrick

Volume 3 – June 2009
THE PRINCE'S CAPTIVE WIFE
by Marion Lennox

Volume 4 – July 2009
THE SHEIKH'S FORBIDDEN VIRGIN
by Kate Hewitt

8 VOLUMES IN ALL TO COLLECT!